Chris was glad to get away from the phone, even though on one level she was glad that Doug had said he'd call again. Her feelings were still mixed up. The night before she'd fallen asleep thinking about Tony.

His kiss had made her feel warm and . . . well, *welcoming* as if it somehow had been something she'd been waiting for. It had made her feel happy. A bubbly kind of happy. They'd talked silly stuff all the way back to camp.

"What's your favorite food?" he'd asked. "Pizza? Mine's strawberries. I could live on strawberries every day for dessert!"

And she'd agreed. She liked Tony. She trusted him. He'd advised her to call her parents. Should she follow his advice?

OFELIA LACHTMAN, a Mexican American, was born and brought up in Los Angeles, where she still lives with her husband. *Campfire Dreams* is her first young adult novel. She is currently working on another one featuring Hispanic characters.

OFELIA LACHTMAN

Campfire Dreams

Keepsake
FROM
CROSSWINDS

===== CROSSWINDS

New York • Toronto • Sydney
Auckland • Manila

First publication August 1987

ISBN 0-373-88006-5

Copyright © 1987 by Ofelia Dumas Lachtman

Printed in the U.S.A.

RL 5.1, IL age 11 and up

Dear Reader:

Welcome to Crosswinds! We will be publishing four books a month, written by renowned authors and rising new stars. You will note that under our Crosswinds logo we are featuring a special line called Keepsake, romantic novels that are sure to win your heart.

We hope that you will read Crosswinds books with pleasure, and that from time to time you will let us know just what you think of them. Your comments and suggestions will help us to keep Crosswinds at the top of your reading list.

Nancy Jackson

Senior Editor
CROSSWINDS BOOKS

Chapter One

Chris Emery took one more look as the bus rounded a curve. A huge castle was silhouetted against the sky. What a great picture that would make! And, wouldn't you know it, she'd just put her camera away. She settled back in the seat and in a moment forgot all about it.

She was thinking of the crisis she had caused at home by insisting on coming here. Mom had been dead set against it and, in a way, so had Dad. But Dad was someone you could reason with, not nervous and overprotective like Mom. Good thing he saw it my way, Chris thought, and pushed the uncomfortable memory aside. She tapped the bus driver on the shoulder. "Are we almost to El Nido?"

"Five more miles," he said.

Farther than she'd thought. Once the bus had left the drizzly June fog of the Southern California coast and started to climb inland, her excitement had grown. And now she couldn't wait to get there.

The driver caught her eye in the rearview mirror. "You a student at one of the fancy schools there?"

"No. I'm going to Camp Whiteoak to be a counselor."

"Sure you're old enough for that?"

She frowned. She knew that her straight blond hair and wide-set gray eyes made her look like a kid. "I'm in high school," she said. "A junior." She swung around to face the window again.

The road now twisted downhill, and within minutes they rode through orange groves on the outskirts of a small town and then on to a sun-baked avenue. The morning was warm, and little shops had spilled their goods onto the sidewalks. Brilliant scarves on racks moved in a sultry breeze, and ceramic pots and oil paintings crowded the doorways. She leaned forward, looking curiously at everything.

The bus curved into a dusty narrow street and stopped. Chris looked around, but there was no station, only a faded green bench by a giant oak. She pulled her camera's leather strap over her shoulder and followed the two other passengers out of the bus. The camp director had said someone from Whiteoak would meet her at the Light Street station, and except for the three of them, the place was deserted.

The driver put the baggage on the bench, and in a few seconds the bus left with a growl and a cloud of exhaust. Chris watched the other passengers walk the short block to the main street. Two small boys on bicycles turned the corner and rode toward her. When they were near, they shouted, ''Hi!'' and waved. She smiled and waved back.

Thank goodness she wouldn't be stuck with that job in L.A. That's just what her mom wanted—to keep her at home like a little kid. Her mom didn't seem to understand how important this job was to her. Well, by the end of summer maybe she'd know whether she even belonged at home. After all, she wasn't their real daughter. Her lip trembled softly, and she bit it until the trembling stopped. I guess it's not fair even to think that, she told herself. Mom and Dad have always treated Susie and me pretty much the same. But who knows? Maybe Susie'll want to move out, too, when she's sixteen. Anyway, I'm where I want to be for the summer—and somebody's bound to come for me soon.

She looked up and down the street and then settled back to wait, watching a spider pull itself toward the top of the oak on an invisible line. It had worked its way up about a foot or so when tires squealed on the hot asphalt and a yellow pickup swerved around the corner. A girl with a mop of curly black hair hung out the window.

"Chris Emery!" she shouted. "Is that you?"

Chris jumped to her feet as the small truck came to a stop beside her.

The girl threw open the door. "Sorry I'm late. I'm Becky Koster. The Whiteoak wagon blew a gasket when I was ready to leave, and anyone else with wheels was using them. Good thing I got hold of Tony."

The guy in the driver's seat got out and walked around the hood to the bench. "I'm Tony Atkinson," he said, his brown eyes glancing at her and then at her luggage. "These your bags?"

She nodded and said, "Thanks for coming for me."

"Glad to." He grinned as he swung her suitcases into the back of the truck. "I'm at Redoak, you know. And even if the lake's between us, our two camps stick pretty close together."

"That's great," Chris said, sliding on to the seat by Becky. "I'm really looking forward to the summer."

Becky smiled. "You'll change your tune when a few hundred little monsters arrive on Saturday. This is a job, remember, and *assistant* counselors don't get pampered."

"Thanks for the warning, but I don't expect to loaf."

Tony started the motor. They drove east toward green-forested hills. Ahead of them a sign said Slow, Narrow Bridge. As they got on the bridge, a car horn blared behind them. Chris twisted to look back. With another loud blare, a white Cadillac swerved to the left and shot forward, squeezing the pickup close to the rail. She gasped as the white car lunged across the small bridge and whipped to the right, inches from their front bumper. She had a blurred impression of a child's face under a blue cap in the rear of the car.

Becky leaned over Chris and shouted out the window, "Creep! You trying to kill us?"

After that they were silent until they rounded a bend by a thicket of cypresses. Tony slowed the car almost to a stop. "There's Whiteoak," he said.

The camp was directly ahead, a cluster of freshly painted tan cottages under oaks and tall thin pines. To her right, above the cottages, Chris could see a high wire fence. Tennis courts? Closer to the gate she saw a stone-lined circle. The fire pit. Beyond the camp, a blue lake stretched for what seemed like miles, its waters rippling lazily against towering green hills. Star Lake. Prettier even than on the camp brochures. The air was cool and sharp with the scent of pine.

The pickup started moving again. They drove between two concrete pillars onto a graveled road that led by a parking lot on one side and a thick stand of pines on the other. Tony pulled up to a wooden building with a sign that said The Lodge. A white Cadillac was parked by the steps.

"What d'ya know?" Becky said. "Killer creep was on his way here. Two days ahead of time. Probably couldn't wait to get rid of his kid."

"Looks that way," Tony said. He put Chris's luggage at the top of the steps on a broad veranda. He grinned at Chris as he said goodbye, then climbed into the truck and drove off.

A screen door slammed behind Chris, and a girl's voice said, "Hey! Was that Doug?"

"No," Becky said, "just Tony. For once driving his car himself."

Chris turned to look at the girl who'd spoken, a pretty blonde with a deep tan. "Doug?" Chris asked. "Is that Doug Harrad you're talking about?"

"Yeah," the blonde said. "He's at Redoak. Know him?"

"Well, sort of. All the girls at Hilldale—that's a girls' school—do. He's the basketball great at Duncan High." And, of course, she'd known he was going to be at Redoak. Maybe it was out of style to have a crush on someone, but she did. On Doug. That was one of the reasons she'd wanted to come here.

The blonde said, "Doug the Great," then grinned at Chris. "I'm Jan Craig. You must be Chris Emery, my cabin mate."

"Am I really? Your cabin mate, I mean. That's great."

Becky shot Chris a glance. "All right, Emery, you're on your own now." She turned to leave, then stopped and spun around. "How'd you manage to get assigned to Twelve?'' she said and, without waiting for an answer, went inside.

"Did I do something?'' Chris asked. "What's she so steamed about?''

Jan shrugged. "That's Becky. You'll get used to her.''

"No way.''

"Suit yourself.'' Jan tilted her head, and her look slid over Chris appraisingly. "Let me guess about you. Crafts. I'll bet you're here to do that crafts stuff.''

"Not that *I* know of. Mostly I fool around with cameras and developing fluid.''

"That's close enough,'' Jan said comfortably. "Come on inside. Training's in the library. I'll show you Cabin Twelve later.''

Chris followed her into a large room with a beamed ceiling and leather couches. Directly across from the entry was a counter marked Registration and at the far side of the room, a large stone fireplace. A blue cap was lying by the hearth, and huddled in one of the wing-backed chairs that flanked the fireplace was a little girl. Her eyes were narrowed under wispy black hair, and her mouth was set in a pout.

"Poor kid,'' Chris whispered to Jan. "She doesn't look very happy.''

"That's an understatement. And, worse luck, she'll probably be one of ours. But come on. Not much left of the morning's training. Let's get there in time to break for lunch." Jan motioned Chris to follow as she moved quickly across the room toward a pair of heavy double doors.

Before Chris reached them she stopped. On the wall beside the right-hand door was a painting of a turreted house on a hill. The house she'd seen from the bus! "Wait, Jan," she said, and walked over to it. "What's this place?"

"That's Teale Mansion—like it used to be. Most of it burned down in the Great Meadows fire."

"But I saw it today."

"Sure, some of it's standing. But most of it's been boarded up more than ten years."

"Nobody lives there then."

"Right. Once in a while film companies from L.A. come up and shoot around it."

Movies. TV. So that was why it seemed familiar.

Jan poked her in the ribs. "What did you think it was? Cabin Twelve?"

Chris didn't see Cabin Twelve until the afternoon's training session was over. It was the farthest from the road and around a curve above the lake that hid it from the main buildings.

She set her suitcases down on the path and rested before climbing the eight steps that led to the door. Inside, the cabin was large and airy, with six metal cots stripped down to mattresses lining each long wall. A locker room and showers that smelled of chlorine were on one side of the dorm. On the other side was a small room— more like a screened-in porch—with two made-up beds.

No trees grew close enough to this side of Twelve to obstruct an overall view of the lake. Close by, clear blue water lapped against huge boulders, and on the far shore, beyond a green-grown mound of an island, were the tree-shaded buildings of Camp Redoak. Chris propped her elbows on the sill and looked across the sun-sparkled water to the boys' camp. Doug Harrad was over there. Would he remember her? Maybe not, but one thing was sure, she was going to make an impression on him this summer or die trying.

One of the made-up cots was already taken. Jan's things, two open suitcases and a pair of discarded jeans, were on it. Chris brought her bags in from the large room, put them on the floor by the other cot and lay down. The mattress was okay, but the pillow was sort of lumpy. You win some, you lose some, she thought philosophically as she sat up and pulled a suitcase onto the bed beside her. But her mood changed when she opened it. Lying right on top of her more or less folded clothes was a bundle of postcards neatly held by two rubber bands. Oh, mother, she thought, there you go again! Still treating me like a child. I'll bet they're even addressed. When she turned them over, she found that she was right. Her face hot with a familiar resentment, she shoved the cards under her clothes and slammed the suitcase shut. Unpacking could wait. There was little time left before the dinner gong was to sound; she'd take a look at the lake.

She left the cabin and walked briskly down the lakeside path to where it ended by a cluster of huge rocks. The late sun slanted through the trees, and the breeze caught the shadows, moving them on the surface of the boulders. The girl with the blue cap was sitting on the top of the largest one. She pushed herself off, sliding down its side to the trail.

Chris watched her repeat the exercise a couple of times and then waved.

The girl looked away.

Chris sat down on a tree stump that jutted out of a mass of periwinkle. "Hi, I'm Chris," she called. When the girl said nothing, she added, "I saw you earlier, when you were waiting for your father in the Lodge."

The girl's chin shot up. "That's not my father," she said. "Him and Marie adopted me." She pulled the blue cap down solidly on her head, scooped up a handful of pebbles and, one by one, tossed them into the lake.

Chris watched the circles of ripples grow and disappear. "They *chose* you," she finally said.

"No," Blue Cap said firmly, "they didn't choose me. My real father's a king," she said in a tone that was now more bragging than belligerent. "He made a deal with them to take care of me."

"Really? Why would he do that?"

"To protect me of course. To keep me away from kidnappers." The blue cap shook impatiently. "I guess you wouldn't understand. You've never been a princess."

"That's true. I've never been a princess. But I'm adopted, too. Maybe I would understand."

The little girl gave her a swift look and once more pulled her cap close to her eyes. "This is sure a crummy camp," she said. "No TV and not one computer game."

"What did you expect? This is an art camp."

The girl shrugged.

Chris got up. "What's your name?" she asked.

"Michelle. 'Course it's not my real name."

"What's your real name?"

The girl's eyes narrowed. "D'ya think I'm dumb or something? I can't tell anybody that."

"Oops. I should've known. All right, I'll just call you Michelle."

"I won't answer. You've gotta call me Mitch."

Chris let out her breath. "Right. See you later, Mitch," she said, and picked her way down to the water. When she found firm footing, she turned. The blue cap was scurrying up the trail, and the dinner bell was ringing.

The dining hall was the largest of all the camp buildings. It was fronted by a cement platform with three stone steps that ran its length. Even before Chris had started up the stairs, the spicy smell of Italian cooking reached her, and her mouth watered. Lasagna, she hoped, but she would settle for spaghetti.

Inside, she hurried past empty round tables to three at the far end of the room that were in use.

There was an empty place next to Jan, and she slid into it. "I'm starved," she whispered.

Jan said, "Me, too. Hope they have something good."

Across the table Becky said, "What's the difference, Jan? You know you'll eat anything."

"Almost anything," Jan said good-naturedly.

Chris noticed that Becky ate very little, even pushing dessert away. Strawberries! Who in her right mind would turn that down?

When dinner was over, Becky jerked her head toward the table behind them. "Hey, Emery," she said. "You ready for our own Mrs. Gotrocks?"

"Who's that?"

"Becky means Mrs. Teale-Lessing," Jan said. "She's the owner of the house in the painting. She also owns Whiteoak."

One of the girls said. "So she owns a girls' camp. That doesn't mean she's rich, does it?"

"Camp Redoak belongs to her, too," Jan answered promptly, "*and* the lake, *and* most of the Great Meadows Valley. I could go on and on, but I see we're about to be interrupted."

At the table near the wall, a pleasant-faced woman rose and tapped her spoon against a glass. "For those of you who don't know, I'm

Margaret Allen, the camp director.'' She added a few words of welcome and then went on to outline the summer's activities. The Grand Finale, she told them, would be the high point of the summer. But that was much later; they would hear more about it. She reminded them that, except for those with whom she had individual conferences, the next afternoon was a free half day for them. Finally she said, ''That's enough from me. Tonight we have the pleasure of hearing from Caroline Teale-Lessing, the owner of this camp, and someone who's been my good friend since we were about your age.''

The woman who rose was forty, maybe, and beautiful. The kind of beauty, Chris thought, that being that age doesn't touch. Her thick blond hair was parted in the middle and pulled back tightly from her oval face. Classy.

Mrs. Lessing's fingertips rubbed the tabletop lightly as her eyes scanned the girls' faces. She spoke briefly, ending with the hope that they, the counselors, would enjoy the summer as much as the campers.

After her talk everyone moved from the dining hall to the library in the Lodge to watch a film of the past summer's events. The old-time counselors applauded and howled when they saw themselves on the screen, and a freckled red-head named Diane took bows when she was shown slipping off the boat dock fully dressed. Chris learned that Diane was her neighbor in Cabin Eleven.

When the film was over, Chris looked around expectantly for Jan. Disappointed not to find her, she started toward the cabin alone, playing her flashlight through the dark pines along the path.

"Hey, Chris! Wait up!"

Chris stopped, and Diane caught up with her. "A bunch of us are driving down to El Nido tomorrow afternoon and—"

"You mean you have a car?" Chris interrupted.

"I've got my brother's gas guzzler for the summer. Want to go with us?"

"I guess I can't," Chris said reluctantly. "My one-to-one with Miss Allen is at three tomorrow."

"Well, another time," Diane said, and ran up the steps to Eleven.

Chris walked up the mountain road slowly, the sun pouring down hot on her head. She got a picture of a squirrel, a peanut held tightly in its forepaws, looking straight at her. He held absolutely still, as if posing, until she clicked the camera, then scurried up a tall pine. She went on, and soon the asphalt became shaded. At a bend in the road she paused. Below her on the lake the sun glistened along the crest of each shallow wave, and the Redoak cabins seemed to be rising as if from a desert mirage. She raised her camera. Looking through the viewfinder, she shifted back and forth to find the best composition.

She didn't hear the car until brakes shrieked. Tires squealed as she scrambled for the side of the road, rolling into the high grass on the slope. On the asphalt a blur of yellow skidded and rammed into the side of the hill.

A door slammed, and she saw Tony dash toward her. "Are you all right?" he asked, grabbing her hand.

"Yes, I think so." She had gotten to her knees, and he pulled her up.

"Are you sure?"

She nodded. "Yes, I'm sure."

"Then," said Tony, expelling his breath in relief, "will you please tell me what you were doing standing in the center of a curving mountain road?"

"I . . . I didn't expect anyone. It seemed so far from anywhere." She gasped and pulled at the camera around her neck. "My camera! I guess it's okay."

"The camera? *The camera?* When I almost killed you?"

"Well, you didn't. And it took every penny I've ever saved to buy this special lens! It's important to me."

"Sure. So's my truck! Look at it. Who knows if it'll get back on the road?"

She saw that the pickup was across the highway, pushed up against an overgrown bank at a crazy angle. "I'm sorry about that," she said.

"So am I. Let's hope it's not stuck." He swung around and walked to the truck, where he slid into the driver's seat. He started the engine and listened to it with a frown on his face.

"Is it all right?"

"Engine sounds okay."

"But how about the rest of it?"

"We'll see." He eased the pickup back on to the road. "No harm done," he said finally, and threw open the door on the passenger's side. "Get in. You must be pretty shaky. I'll give you a lift."

She pulled herself into the cab. Without any warning, her knees had begun to shake.

Tony shifted the truck's gears and let it move forward. "Didn't mean to be so rough," he said, "but you really scared me."

"Don't apologize. It was my fault. That was dumb, standing in the middle of the road to take a picture."

"So that's what you were doing! Well, did you get it?"

She shook her head. "There wasn't time."

"Sorry. I *would* have to come along just then."

"Don't be so nice. I'm the one to blame. You could've been killed, too, you know."

"I wasn't, so forget the whole thing. When are you due back at camp?"

"Not until three."

"Good. If you'll go for a ride with me, I'll show you a great place to take pictures."

"I'd like that."

They rode in silence through thickets of young trees. After a few miles the trees thinned and the narrow highway wound steeply by the edge of a hill. Tony stopped the pickup in a graveled clearing bordered on the cliffside by a low stone fence. Showing above huge, rambling shrubs next to the clearing were the mossy roofs of two round towers and the blackened tops of several enormous chimneys.

"Hey," she said, "this is the place in the painting at the Lodge."

"The old Teale house," Tony said. "Inhabited by birds, mostly pigeons, maybe bats and a ghost or two. But that's not what we came to see." He jumped out and opened her door. "Come on," he said, taking her hand. "Get a load of this." They walked to the stone wall.

In the early afternoon sun the mountains that rimmed the bowl-like valley beneath them were ribboned in purple and tan. Below the mountains, on the floor of the basin, a church steeple glinted above a clustering storybook village. And, like an old-fashioned quilt, a checkerboard of groves spread from the town onto the hillsides.

Chris stood still for a few moments, looking down on the deep valley. Then she drew in her breath and turned away.

"Hey, Chris, you're white as a sheet. Something wrong?"

"I don't know. It's weird. I know this place. I've known it for a long time. It's the valley in my dream."

Chapter Two

Funny," Chris said. Her heart, still beating wildly, made her voice shake. "It's really funny to be standing here wide awake."

"You look as if you've seen a ghost," Tony said. "That dream of yours must've been more like a nightmare."

"It was. I mean, it is. I still have it. I've had it for as long as I can remember."

Tony leaned back against the wall. "What's the dream about?"

"It's a chase. In it I'm a little girl, and I'm running in front of a huge, bright light that's coming at me, ready to swallow me up." She paused, frowning at the memory.

"So what happens?"

"The usual. I stumble and fall and scream because now it's going to catch me. But all of a sudden I'm safe. Held in someone's arms. A woman, I think. And we're standing at the top of a high hill exactly like this one, facing mountains exactly like those mountains, looking down on a valley exactly like this." She had been looking at the mountains as she spoke. Now she glanced at Tony. "Crazy, huh?"

"Maybe not. You probably knew this place. Don't people dream about places they've seen?"

"But I've never been here before. Not as far as I know."

"That's crazy," he said, a small furrow of concentration between his eyes. "Was there more to your dream?"

"No. I'd wake up about then—screaming, sometimes—and Mom or Dad would be sitting on the edge of my bed."

"So what do they say about it?"

"Not much. But then I didn't tell them much. For some reason, I had trouble talking about it. Hey, I'm sorry. I didn't mean to unload on you."

"You didn't. I like to talk with you."

She smiled at him, and their eyes met. Quickly she dropped her glance and pressed her hands against the fence. The roughness of the stones felt good, and the breeze was warm on her cheeks.

After a while she said, "Has this valley ever been written up? You know, in newspapers or magazines, maybe with pictures I could've seen?"

"I doubt it. There's nothing special about Little Valley. Unless it was the fire."

"What fire?"

"The Great Meadows fire. But that was too long ago. Even if it had made the city papers, I doubt you would've been interested. Too busy with your building blocks. At least I was then."

"Well, that's that, isn't it?"

Tony shrugged. "Of course, there could have been something I don't know about. Say," he said, his face brightening, "I'll tell you who would know if there was. My aunt. She runs the Crown Hotel down in El Nido, and she hears about everything that goes on."

"You mean you live around here?"

"Sure. Born here. But, say, about my aunt. I could take you to see her. When's your next free time?"

"I won't know until later this afternoon." There was a flurry of wings as several pigeons came batting out of one of the towers. "We're bothering the tenants," she said, grinning. "Maybe we'd better go. Anyway, I'd better not be late for my meeting."

"You'll make it with time to spare. But, okay, let's go."

They were about to get in the pickup when a long chauffeur-driven car pulled alongside. The driver, wearing a crisp uniform, got out and opened the rear door. Caroline Teale-Lessing leaned toward them. "It *is* you, Tony. I thought I recognized your truck."

"Hi, Mrs. Lessing. Nice to see you."

"I'm glad to see you, too, Tony," Mrs. Lessing said, "I was going to stop in and see your father later, but you'll save me a trip if you'll give him a message."

"Glad to."

She looked over Tony's head to the towers beyond. "I'm here for a last goodbye. We're finally going to tear down the old house."

"That wonderful old house?" Chris blurted. "Oh, how sad!"

"Yes, it is," Mrs. Lessing said. A shadow crossed her face.

Tony shot Chris a glance and said, "This is Chris Emery from Whiteoak, Mrs. Lessing."

The woman nodded and turned back to Tony. "Please tell your father that the wreckers are coming at the end of July. Anything he wants from the house is his. The carving around the library fireplace. Some of it's still left."

"That's great! Dad'll be—"

"Tell him, too," Mrs. Lessing interrupted, and Chris wondered if she'd even heard Tony, "that Santiago has been told to expect him. You know how that good man guards this place."

"Yeah," Tony said with a smile, "but only from strangers." He ran his hand lightly across the limousine's hood. "Señor Marcos treats me fine. Even lets me practice my Spanish on him."

"He's lonely," Mrs. Lessing said. "It's not easy to be alone. And ever since..." Her thought hung unfinished in the warm afternoon air. She sighed. "Well, I'd better be on my way. Nice to have met you, Chris," she said with a faint little smile.

Riding back to camp, Chris tried to sort out her feelings. She closed her eyes, willing the subject out of her mind, but images of the deep valley and of the velvety green roofs of Teale Mansion kept crowding in. She had recognized them. But how? Surely, when she'd shown her folks the camp brochures, they would have said something if they'd all been up here together. It was too confusing. She was glad when Tony pulled up at the Whiteoak gate.

"Hey, Emery, where've you been?" Becky was sitting at the far side of the veranda on a bench that faced the road, her feet propped on the rail.

Chris climbed the steps and said, "Hi, Becky, I thought you'd gone with the others."

"Sure you did." Becky, her dark eyes flashing, got up. "Where've you been with Tony?"

"We went to the lookout by Teale Mansion."

"To admire the view, I'll bet."

Ignoring Becky's remark, Chris glanced at her watch. "Gotta run. Miss Allen's waiting," she said.

By four o'clock Chris's conference with the camp director was practically over. Miss Allen rose and handed Chris a sheet of paper. "I think we've covered everything," she said. "That's the program for the week. We have you scheduled for a Shutterbug Hike on Wednesday along with Diane."

"Diane. I'm glad of that. I'll take all the help I can get."

Miss Allen shook her head and smiled. "Relax, Chris, you'll do fine. We want you to enjoy your summer. It won't be all work, you know. There'll be free days, too. And there's a lot to see around here. Great Meadows and Little Valley are beautiful."

"I know," Chris said. She hoped Miss Allen hadn't heard the uneasiness in her voice.

Chris was humming as she walked to the dining hall to begin the Shutterbug Hike. Nine girls with red caps and Mitch, still wearing the old blue one, were waiting on the long steps. All had cameras hanging around their necks.

"Where's your Whiteoak cap, Mitch?" Chris asked.

"I lost it. Anyway, I hate red."

"Try to find it, say by bedtime."

In a few minutes Becky came out of the Lodge door and ran down the steps toward them.

Chris asked, "Have you seen Diane?"

"No, and neither will you. She's subbing at the pool."

"But she's supposed to go with me." Chris tried to hold back her disappointment.

"I'm taking her place," Becky said. "Not that I want to."

"Do you have to then?"

"Of course I do. We've got that stupid buddy system." She looked up at the sky. "This hike ought to be called off, anyway. Looks like rain to me."

"Whatever you think," Chris said, "but the kids will really be disappointed if we cancel."

"Oh, I'd cancel anyway, but it's not up to me. The hike's on unless we're told otherwise. Come on, Emery, I'll show you the trail and keep them in line. You do the rest." She turned to the girls. "Front and center and listen!" They gathered around her and she laid out her rules. Then she said, "All right, let's move." She shooed them toward a path that led into the hills.

Chris and Mitch brought up the rear. The trail, which curved along the lake, was bordered by young trees. Every now and then through the thickets, Chris caught a glimpse of blue water. After a while the path took a sharp turn, and the lake lay spread out below them. There was a gentle breeze ruffling the water, and the ripples sparkled with sunlight. The island in the center was an emerald green, and the red roofs of the boys' camp showed through the trees like the brilliant plumage of exotic birds. "It's beautiful," Chris said.

Becky stared silently down at the lake. Shoving her hands into the pockets of her shorts, she said, "Just don't look at Moon Island at night."

Someone asked, "Why not?"

"You might get scared, that's why."

"Doesn't look spooky to me," Mitch said.

"Me, neither," Shana added. Curly-headed Shana had become Mitch's shadow and echo.

Chris looked up at Becky. Was she just trying to scare the kids? Yet her face was entirely serious as she slid down the leaf-strewn soil of the bank to the trail.

Now the path led away from the lake, winding upward between thick, wooded slopes. Here and there slanting shafts of sunlight spotlighted drifts of pine needles and cones. When they came to where the trails branched, Chris looked up the right-hand trail. The trees grew sparser as the path rose, and high above them she could see bright patches of sunshine.

"Let's go this way," she called. "There's light up there."

Becky said, "That place? Forget it. That's the old castle."

Mitch stopped in her tracks and whirled around. "A *real* castle? Let's go!"

"Do you mean Teale Mansion?" Chris asked.

"Yes, and we're not going there." Becky waved to a darkening ribbon of sky showing above the hills. "Look at those clouds. We'll get caught in a storm if we make too many stops."

"If it's a castle," Mitch said, "I'd like to see it."

"Not when I'm running the show," Becky said.

Chris motioned her to one side. "This trail's no good for photographs. Even pros would have trouble here."

"Well, don't cry about it," Becky said. "We'll soon be at Trail's End. There's a monument to an Indian chief there, and rest rooms, and a drinking fountain. You can take pictures of all of them if you want."

"Thanks. We will if there's nothing more interesting," Chris said crossly.

Now the trees were larger and more widely spaced, and presently they saw large areas of sunlight at the edge of the forest. In another few minutes they reached a clearing.

The girls scattered for the rest rooms and the drinking fountain. Then they shoved and slid their way onto picnic benches for a snack, their red caps making a line of bright color against the darkening forest. But something was missing—a touch of blue.

"Mitch!" Chris called and got no answer. "Anyone seen Mitch?"

"Not me. Me, neither." No one, it seemed, had seen Mitch for some time.

Becky said, "Thought you were watching her, Emery."

"So did I. Maybe she's in the john." Chris made a quick search of both the rest rooms and then around the clearing. She walked a little way into the woods, calling Mitch's name, but soon gave up and went back to the picnic table.

"Mitch isn't here, Becky. What do we do now?" she asked.

"Worry." Becky shivered. "And then go back to camp for help."

"Help? What do we need help for? Why don't we take a look at the old mansion?"

"I told you I wouldn't go near that place."

"Okay. You wait with the girls. I'll go after her."

"Up there? Alone?"

"Why not? What's up there? Just an old house and a caretaker."

"A crazy caretaker."

"Crazy? That's not what I heard. I think you're imagining things."

"Doesn't make any difference if I am. I'm in charge, remember, and we're supposed to work in pairs."

"All right, then. Let's all go."

"Not on your life. We're all heading back to camp."

Chris shook her head. "Not me. Not without Mitch."

"Suit yourself."

Becky called to the girls and, for once silent, they scurried to get their stuff together.

Chris watched them leave the picnic tables and head toward the trail. "All right, go ahead!" she shouted fiercely. "I'm going to Teale Mansion!"

Chapter Three

The path was tortuous, twisting a slow way through the thick woods. Once in a while in the treetops, Chris heard the flurry of wings, but otherwise the shadowy forest was quiet. Then, in the distance, she heard a low rumbling that rolled above the trees. The air stood still, as if waiting, then became cold. Chris tried to climb faster, but the trail was covered with layers of pine needles and she had to step carefully to keep from sliding. She was breathing heavily when she finally neared the top.

Here logs formed steps in the trail, making the climb easier. Through thinning trees she saw the turrets of Teale Mansion. This must be the other side of the old house, the side opposite the lookout Tony had taken her to, she speculated. Before she reached the top, lightning flashed beyond the rim of the mountains and thunder rolled angrily.

She climbed the last step and found herself at the edge of the open area she had seen from below. Across the clearing, about fifty feet away from where she stood, a small cottage nestled against the tall overgrown shrubbery that separated it from the larger house. Freshly painted, white with yellow shutters, it was like a splash of sunlight in the murky afternoon. Lamplight glowed from one of its windows. The caretaker's house, of course. Should she knock?

Chris was still hesitating when thunder cracked above her. For a second there was quiet, then, a heavy downpour pelted the treetops and pummeled her head and shoulders. She raced around a vegetable garden and across stepping stones to the shelter of the cottage porch. The door was open, a rectangle of light falling on the porch floor. She rapped loudly on the screen door's frame. "Hello!" she called. "Hello! Is anyone home?"

A flash of lightning caught her by surprise. She held her breath as a sound like heavy steps came from inside the little house, then expelled it in relief as a couple of pinecones bounced from the roof to the ground. Then, through the noise of the storm, she heard a voice.

"What are you doing here?" An old man in earth-stained jeans stood at the edge of the woods. He was carrying a hoe, and when he started toward her, she shrank against the railing.

He placed the hoe on the floor of the porch, wiped his wet face on his shirtsleeve and repeated, "What are you doing here?"

She gave a silly, nervous laugh. "I'm looking for a little girl wearing a blue cap. Have you seen her?"

"It is possible," he said, his dark eyes expressionless under white hair that was thick and wet, "entirely possible. But, if so, I can't recall when. Is it important that you know?"

"Of course it's important. I'm in charge of her, and she's wandered off. And I'm afraid she might be lost in this storm."

"Ah, that is sad," he said, "to lose someone. And you have been looking for her for a long time, yes?"

"Only half an hour or so, and the sooner I find her, the better. But in this rain..." She smiled weakly. "I'm Chris Emery from Whiteoak. I'm a counselor there. Are you the caretaker?"

He straightened his shoulders beneath his clinging wet shirt and said with great dignity, "I am Santiago Marcos, *señorita*, at your service."

"Well, I hope you don't mind my nosing around. I'm pretty sure Mitch came up here. We got all the way to Trail's End, though, before we missed her. I can't imagine how she got away."

"It happens," he said. *"Los niños tienen mas salidas que un cerco viejo."*

"That's Spanish, isn't it? What does it mean?"

"Poorly translated, it says that children have more exits than an ancient fence. But you're wet, *señorita*. Come in, come in."

"No. I'll wait right here."

He nodded and went inside, returning quickly with a towel, which he held out to her. While she dried herself, he leaned over the railing, studying the sky.

"The gods are angry," he muttered. "But only just a little. The rain will soon pass."

"I hope you're right. I've got to find Mitch. She'll be sopping wet."

"Maybe not, maybe not," he said, and went into the house.

By the time Chris had blotted the water from her hair and clothes, the rain had almost stopped and the sun was pushing through the clouds. She spread the towel on the railing and was about to knock when the caretaker appeared at the door.

"I think I know where your *chiquita* might be," he said.

"Where? Where?"

"Come with me." He walked toward the high wall of shrubbery between the cottage and the mansion.

"Where are you going?" Chris asked.

"To find your little one." He passed through an opening in the hedge.

Chris followed him at a distance on a narrow walkway that was bordered on one side by the enormous hedge and on the other by the wall of the great house.

The old man was waiting for her under a latticework arch. He was holding open a wooden gate.

Again she hesitated. "Where are we going?"

"See for yourself," he said softly. "There is nothing to fear."

She felt herself blush. Had she been that obvious? She took a few quick steps into the archway, but there she stopped.

She was looking into a play yard, one carpeted with green grass and scattered with colorful flower beds. There was everything here: swings, bars, a seesaw. In the center, enclosed by a low, scalloped fence, a playhouse painted bright orange glistened in the sunlight. What a place for kids! But what kids? Tony had said that no one lived at Teale Mansion except birds and bats, and maybe a ghost or two. What was a play yard, a brand-new, well-kept play yard, doing here? She shot the old caretaker a questioning glance, but he said nothing. She walked toward the playhouse, and as she did, the door flew open.

Mitch stuck her head out. "Chris! Hey, Chris, is that you?"

"It's me, all right, and am I glad to see you!"

"La chiquita," Señor Marcos mumbled. "Just as I thought."

"Mitch, are you okay?"

"Course. Isn't this all neat, Chris? I just knew it would be."

Chris looked at Mitch's grinning face under a dry blue cap, and annoyance drove out her relief. "Doesn't matter what you knew, Mitch," she said angrily, "you'd no business to go off alone!"

"You're mad at me," Mitch said.

"Darned right! What do you expect when you run off and worry everybody? If it hadn't been for Señor Marcos, I wouldn't have found you."

"I wasn't lost! I wanted to see the castle, and you and Becky wouldn't let me."

Chris gave her a threatening glance. She looked around at the high wire fence that enclosed the play yard, then turned to the old man. "Is there a gate over there? Near the road?" When he nodded, she said, "We'll go that way, then. Thanks for all your help."

Chris tapped Mitch's shoulder. "Come on. They'll be waiting for us at Whiteoak."

"Why can't we go the way we came?"

"Because I'm not sure I can find the way we came."

"I can."

"Maybe you can, but I'm not going to take a chance on getting lost. We'll go by the highway. It may be longer, but it's safer."

"I think that's dumb."

"I don't care what you think. Just come on." Taking a glum-faced Mitch by the hand, Chris made her way through the bushes that lined the asphalt road.

"Don't see why we had to hurry," Mitch grumbled. "The rain's stopped. I didn't even get a chance to use the swings."

"You shouldn't have been there to begin with."

"But nobody was using those things. There was everything there, 'cept a slide, of course."

"Doesn't matter," Chris snapped. "You were trespassing. Besides, there *was* a slide."

"Uh-uh. There was that playhouse, and a see-saw, *and* swings, but I didn't see any old slide."

"But there was one. Shaped like a shoe."

"There wasn't!" Mitch stopped in her tracks. "Come on, let's go back and I'll show you!"

"No way," Chris said, pulling at the legs of her wet shorts. "I've got to get back to camp and get out of these clothes."

"A slide like a shoe," Mitch muttered. "You sure get funny ideas." She threw her a disgusted look and ran on ahead.

Above them a bird chirped. A ripple of song came from one tree, then another, until finally the forest was filled with singing. Chris splashed through a rain puddle, pushed her wet hair away from her face and caught up with Mitch. They walked together, saying nothing.

A couple of cars came up the road from the direction of Whiteoak, and Chris watched them approach, praying someone had been sent for them. But in each instance she was disappointed. They rounded curve after curve of the highway, each time finding only more asphalt stretching out before them.

Mitch's shoulders slumped. "When are we gonna get there?" she whined.

"Don't know. Just be glad it's downhill."

When Chris heard the hiss of tires behind her, she turned to look. It was the yellow pickup. "Tony!" she yelled.

The truck came to a squealing halt, and the door flew open. It wasn't Tony. The boy hunched over the wheel was Doug Harrad.

"You're not wet or anything, are you?" he asked with a grin.

For one crazy moment Chris wanted to turn and run. Instead, she said, "No, I always look this way."

"Get in," he said.

Mitch pushed by Chris and scrambled onto the seat next to him. He waved his hand impatiently. "Don't just stand there. Aren't you heading for Whiteoak?"

Chris nodded and got into the cab. The pickup moved forward.

"I'm Doug Harrad," he said, looking at her above Mitch's head. "And you?"

"Chris Emery," she answered, and slid down in the seat.

"She's my counselor," Mitch volunteered. "She comes from Los Angeles, just like me."

"L.A., huh? Where?"

"West L.A.," Chris said reluctantly. "On Webster."

"Really? Duncan High?"

"No."

"Well, then, where?"

"I go to Hilldale Girls—"

"I've got it," he cut in. "I've been wondering why you looked familiar. I met you at Deb Kendal's, didn't I?" He shot her a quick sidelong glance. "But you looked different then."

"I know," Chris said, "dry." She'd hoped to make an impression on Doug, but not this way! However, she began to feel better as she listened to Mitch bombard him with questions. By the time they reached Whiteoak, she was feeling quite relaxed.

At the Lodge they met Jan coming down the steps. "You back already?" she said. "Where are the others?"

"They must've ducked in out of the rain somewhere," Chris said, but Jan wasn't listening. She was racing toward the road.

"Hey, Doug!" she called, "hang on! I want to see you."

"All right, Mitch," Chris said, "let's go face Miss Allen."

"What for?"

"You know what for. You know the rules."

"Do we have to?"

"Yes, we have to." There was a burst of laughter from the road and Jan's voice saying, "Cut that out, you dimwit." Chris swung around on the top step. "Tell you what, Mitch," she said. "We'll come back later. I want a hot shower and dry clothes before I do anything."

"Me, too," Mitch said, as she jumped down the steps and started up the path.

Before they rounded the turn that led to Cabin Twelve, they heard shouts. "Hey, Chris! Hey, Mitch!" Coming down the lakeside trail was the rest of the picture-taking crew.

"Boy, am I wet," Shana whimpered, her curls clinging to her pouting face in soggy little wisps. "We almost drowned getting down to the pavilion."

Mitch put her arm on Shana's shoulder, and they trotted off toward the cabin.

Becky, hands on her hips, was barking orders to the other campers. "Report to your living group leaders. Don't any of you forget! And get into dry clothes." She turned to Chris. "I see you found her."

"Actually, I didn't find her. Señor Marcos did."

"You saw him?"

"Sure."

"What'd he do?"

"Invited me in," Chris said, a note of satisfaction creeping into her voice.

"You didn't go!"

"Of course not. But I wasn't afraid. There's something really nice about him."

"Yeah, sure." Becky looked at her speculatively. "Mary last year. Now you. He's hung up on blondes. I'd watch out for him if I were you."

Chris looked at her closely. There was a note of conviction in Becky's voice, the same note she had heard when earlier Becky had warned the kids about Moon Island.

"Can I talk to you, Chris?" The whisper was Mitch's.

Chris shot up in bed. "What's wrong?"

"Nothing."

"Then what are you doing up?"

"I can't sleep. I . . . I wanted to . . . I'm sorry . . . you know, that I ran away."

"It's okay, Mitch. If you're sorry, that's enough."

Mitch stood up. "I'm glad you're not mad at me."

"I'm not," Chris said, "so go back to sleep."

"I will." Mitch took a step or two, then turned. "Honest, Chris. Honest, I didn't see any old slide. But, anyway, I'm sorry I said you had funny ideas."

"It's okay. Go on back to sleep." Chris watched Mitch pad into the dorm.

Chris slid under the blankets but almost instantly threw them off. She leaned against the windowsill and stared out into the lake at the shadowy mound that was Moon Island. The moon slid behind a cloud, dimming the outline of the island and the trees, filling the night with dense, shapeless gray. From deep in the pines an owl called, "Who-o-o-o," and like an echo, called again.

Chapter Four

As the days went by, Chris found that her ride with Tony to the Teale Mansion lookout began to seem part of the dream, her same old dream. She was almost surprised to find a note in her box from him almost two weeks later.

His aunt at the Crown Springs Hotel, Tony wrote, couldn't think of anything earthshaking about El Nido or Little Valley that might have appeared in a magazine or newspaper, but she would be happy to talk with Chris, anyway. How about Sunday? Did she have free time coming?

He'd come by for her about one unless she called.

So at one-thirty on Sunday afternoon Chris stood with Tony in the warm sunshine by the Crown Springs Hotel. They started down the graveled drive toward a pair of stone lions at the foot of a flight of steps. Chris stopped in her tracks.

"Tony," she said. "Those lions. I've seen them before."

"Figures. You must have been here before."

Dropping Tony's hand, Chris walked over to the steps and stared thoughtfully at the lions. "There's something different about them," she said finally, "but even so..."

Tony stood silently with her for another minute, and then they went up the stairs and stopped in front of a massive double door. It was set in the middle of a broad veranda. Cushioned wicker chairs were scattered on the porch. A stoutish man in a golf shirt and a woman with immense glasses were reading the Sunday paper. The man looked up and smiled briefly. Inside, the lobby had more wicker furniture. A door marked Josephine Blair, Manager opened, and a slight, white-haired woman stepped out.

"Well, Tony," she said, smiling, "right on time. Come on in."

"Aunt Josie, this is Chris Emery, the girl I told you about."

"Hi, Mrs. Blair. Nice to meet you." Chris walked to the older woman and held out her hand.

Josephine Blair took Chris's hand in both of hers and nodded approvingly. Then she removed her glasses. "There, that's better. Now I can really see you."

Chris felt her cheeks grow red as the older woman studied her face.

Mrs. Blair took a step back. "Forgive my rudeness, young lady, but I could swear I've seen you before." Then, with a little frown and a shake of the head, she said, "No, no, pay no attention. This happens to me often. One sees so many people in the hotel business. After a time, faces tend to blur into one another."

"Guess they would," Chris said. "But maybe you have seen me before. I keep bumping into things I seem to remember. And I've seen Little Valley—in my dreams, that is—for years. Maybe Tony told you about it."

"Didn't tell her anything," Tony said. "Thought you'd want to."

Mrs. Blair gave a little snort and smiled affectionately at Tony. "He's not much of a talker, you know. Well, come in, come in." She led them into a small room, walked around a large oak desk and pulled open louvered blinds. Sunlight poured in, making the white walls glisten and the patterned flowers of a blue Oriental rug spring into life. She motioned to a chair. "Now. *You'd* better tell me about it. Sit down, sit down, both of you."

Chris told her about the valley and then, awkwardly, about her dream. She soon discovered that Mrs. Blair was as easy to talk with as Tony. It wasn't long until she found herself telling about Mitch and the slide.

Mrs. Blair said, "The little girl was right, you know. There is no slide there—not now."

"What do you mean, 'not now'?"

"Well, long ago there was a slide."

"You mean it wasn't there the other day?"

"Hasn't been for years." Josephine Blair sat back, almost lost in the leather chair. "After the Great Meadows tragedy, Santiago Marcos, Caroline Teale-Lessing's caretaker, rebuilt the play yard. On his own, you know. Caroline wanted nothing to do with that house after Katy was lost. But old Santiago left out the slide. It must've been too difficult for him. It was shaped like the nursery rhyme shoe, with the figures of the woman and her children embossed on its side. Caroline gave Katy everything, perhaps too much of everything.''

"Wait, Mrs. Blair. You're throwing things too fast at me. Who's Katy?"

"Caroline's daughter. She was just a little girl when . . . when it all took place."

"When what took place? The fire, you mean?"

"That's right, my dear. The fire took the little girl and her nurse."

"That's awful," Chris said. "How did it happen?"

"We don't really know. Santiago's wife, Celia, who was Katy's nurse, must have died with her. At least we think so."

Tony said, "They never found them. Isn't that the story?"

"That's what made it so bad. Caroline spent thousands of dollars on private detectives, but they didn't turn up a clue. Then she offered a substantial reward. Nothing came of that. All of this took a long time, and it took its toll on both of them. Caroline finally stopped grieving. As for Santiago . . . he's never been quite the same."

"Sure, he talks about them a lot," Tony said, "but he's okay."

"How long ago was all this?" Chris asked.

"Thirteen years," Mrs. Blair said. "None of us can forget. More than twenty people died, most of them people we knew well . . ."

She leaned forward. "You know, Chris, people have been coming here for years. This is a resort area. Hotels, hot springs, health farms, and at least two campgrounds in the State Park above Star Lake. Perhaps, as a little girl, you were here. There's nothing so strange about that, is there?"

"I guess not," Chris said without conviction. Why hadn't her parents mentioned it to her? Neither of them had exactly encouraged her to come to Camp Whiteoak, but then neither had they said anything about having ever been there.

Mrs. Blair cleared her throat. "Well," she said, "well, well." And then, briskly, "Let's have something cold to drink." She poured icy lemonade from a tall cut-glass pitcher that was waiting on a nearby table and made polite conversation about the town and the hotel.

The things she talked about were interesting, and she was friendly, but it was clear to Chris that she had closed the door on the other subject. Chris nodded and smiled at the right places, but said very little. Finally she said, "You must have lots of important things to do, Mrs. Blair. Maybe we ought to go."

"Yes, we should," Tony said. "I've got to be back at camp soon. Becky will be waiting. Tryouts today for the Grand Finale."

Chris stood up. "Thanks for all your help, Mrs. Blair. At least I learned one thing. I've been here before."

Chris was quiet on the way back to camp, and Tony didn't try to talk to her. He whistled softly as he drove, now and again slanting a quick look her way. She smiled at him. He was comfortable to be with, even though he wasn't as fascinating as Doug. She waved goodbye to him at the gate and ran up the path to the counselors' shack.

Magazines were strewn on the low table and slip-covered couch, and a couple of empty Coke cans lay on the floor, but no one was there. Cabin Twelve was empty, too. Chris sat on her bunk and leafed through an old *Redbook*. Finally she tossed it aside, and taking her camera from her locker, she headed for the lakeside trail.

Walking felt good, and she went farther than she had planned. At a turn in the path she found herself above a narrow wooded inlet whose waters lapped against a small dock and an open octagonal building. This had to be the pavilion where Becky and the kids had sat out the storm. A breeze stirred the surface of the lake, and sparks of sunlight tipped the rippled water. She stopped walking to watch a rowboat make its way toward the cove. The boat moved steadily. At that moment the sunlight glistened from the head of the rower, and she recognized the thick white hair. Señor Marcos. She decided to get a close-up before she lost the light.

Chris hurried up the path, looking for a way down to the pavilion. She found it just below the trail to Teale Mansion, reaching the pavilion just as the old man was tying up the boat. Inside the summerhouse she kneeled on a narrow seat that lined the walls and watched him mount a ladder on the side of the wooden dock. When he reached the top, she leaned over the railing and waved. "Hello, Señor Marcos!"

Shielding his eyes with his hands, he raised his head. "Where have you been?" he asked as he started up the rough stone steps that curved to the open building.

She hung over the railing. "What? Me? Are you talking to me?"

He stopped and looked up at her again. "Of course," he said. "We've been waiting for you. We've been waiting for a long time, Katy."

"My name's not Katy, Señor Marcos. It's Chris, Chris Emery, remember?"

Señor Marcos walked to the built-in bench and sat down, his hands hanging limply between his knees. "Foolish old man," he said, shaking his head. "Sometimes I think I live only in my dreams."

"I know about dreams. They can be awfully real."

"Yes."

"Frightening, too."

"Perhaps. But one must not lose them. *Nada es mas triste que la muerte de un sueño.*" He leaned back against the railing. "Nothing is sadder than the death of a dream," he translated for her.

She looked away. He had seemed strong when rowing the boat, but now he seemed old and fragile. Chris restrained her impulse to reach out to console him. Instead, she tightened her fingers around the edge of the bench and looked up at the domed ceiling, where torn cobwebs clung to the boards and the blackened light fixture.

Beside her, Señor Marcos sat silently, his hands clasped together, his eyes closed. Finally he opened them and turned to her. "Katy will be about your age," he said. "Taller than Celia by now. And why not? After all, Celia is no larger than a child herself." A long sigh escaped him.

"Señor Marcos, you called me Katy. Why? Do I look like her?"

"Yes, you look like her. Her hair was long and golden like yours. But Katy's eyes are gray, while yours are not."

Mine are gray, too, Chris thought, even if this shirt makes them look blue.

A shadow crept over the old man's wrinkled face. "Celia and Katy went walking twice on that day. They were looking for Katy's necklace, and the little one cried because they didn't find it. So Celia held her and rocked her and promised they would look again after lunch." His eyebrows drew together. "A long time ago." He shook his head as if to clear it and abruptly got up, moving swiftly toward the arched entry.

"Don't go. Please, don't go." Some impulse...no, not an impulse, a need, made her beg him. She reached for her camera. "Would you let me take your picture?"

"*My* picture? You want a picture of this old man?" Señor Marcos threw his head back and laughed.

To her surprise, it was the laugh of a young, strong man. Yet only a moment ago he had seemed so sad. "Of course I want it. Wouldn't have asked otherwise."

"In that case, *señorita*," he said, "it would be rude to say no."

He stood where she asked, an indulgent little smile playing around his mouth as Chris snapped the pictures. Then he turned and started up the path. She watched him trudge up the hill and disappear into the trees.

Once more Chris sat alone on the bench and listened to the rhythmic lapping of the water splashing the rocks below. After all, she had been lucky, she thought. Mom and Dad had found her. They'd told her she'd been wandering alone on a highway, a grimy towheaded little girl in torn cotton pants. She had been clutching a broken silver chain. They'd said they'd fallen in love with her right then. Then, when months had gone by and no one had claimed her, they'd adopted her.

She still had that chain and the little crystal heart that dangled from it. As a kid she used to stare at the heart, hoping that, like a fortune-teller's ball, it would tell her something about herself. She'd worn it night and day until she was eight or nine. It had been more than a necklace to her. She stiffened. *Necklace.* The old man had said Katy had lost a necklace. What if it were a chain with a crystal heart? What if... She turned and stared at the glistening surface of the lake. Wouldn't it be funny if she were Katy Teale-Lessing? Funny? No, it wouldn't be funny at all. She swiveled around and rubbed her arms. She actually had goose bumps! Katy Teale-Lessing? Ridiculous! Katy was dead. She'd been lost in the fire. But what if she hadn't been? What if she'd wandered off and someone had found her? Chris shivered. It all seemed to fit.

From the very first day that she'd come to the Great Meadows Valley, she had been running into—well, what were they?—not exactly memories, more like hints of something locked up in her mind. Like the valley she'd dreamed of so many times. Like the turrets of Teale Mansion. The slide, too. A couple of hours ago, the lions at the hotel. And just now the things Señor Marcos had said. If only she could talk to her father! But she couldn't call home. Her argument with her mother had driven a wedge between them, a cold, sharp separation that was like nothing she had ever felt before.

Mom had said, "Call us if you need us, Chrissy."

"I'm a big girl, now, Mom," she had replied. "There's no way I'll need to call you. You won't hear from me all summer long. You'll see."

False pride? Maybe. But she wouldn't call them. There would be no use in asking them more questions. They'd already told her all they knew.

She had to talk to someone. Not her folks. Not Señor Marcos. He was more mixed up than she was. Jan? No, no. Jan would probably say, "Tell Mrs. Lessing," and she couldn't do that, either. Suddenly it came to her. *Tony*. Tony knew everyone in town. She would have to ask Tony to help her.

Chapter Five

Give me a minute to get my head on straight."

Tony gave Chris a questioning look but said
nothing as they walked to the end of the dock.
They sat on the edge of the pier, their legs dan-
gling above the water for a couple of minutes and
then Chris swallowed hard and plunged in.

"Did I ever tell you I'm adopted?"

"No. So?"

"So this. Mom and Dad got me when I was
three and nobody, nobody at all, ever found out
who my real parents were. You're going to laugh,
maybe, but I think, at last, I have."

"What do you mean?"

There was a splash in the water behind them, and they turned to find Val, an assistant counselor, and a group of kids in bathing suits at the edge of the lake. Chris frowned. "Let's go somewhere else," she said to Tony.

"Sure. There's a place below the lake trail I call the Bleachers." He got up and held out his hand. "It's not too far."

"Good. I'll tell you what I mean on the way."

They took the lakeside trail for a while and pushed and slid through a thick stand of pines to the water's edge. A cluster of huge rocks, one of them as flat as a bench, clung to the embankment near an opening in the trees that gave a wide view of the lake. By the time they had climbed up to them and were settled, Chris had almost finished telling him about her talk with Santiago Marcos.

"See what I mean? He told me Katy's eyes were gray. So are mine. And Katy had that necklace. So did I. It could be the same one. But that's not the main thing. It's all those places I remember. Maybe it's crazy, but everything seems to fit."

"Wow," Tony said. "That's some story. What about your folks? Shouldn't you talk to them? Do you get along with them?"

Chris felt her face grow hot. "Sure, I get along with them," she said. "They're the best parents anyone could want, and what's more, they wanted me!" She let out a long breath. "The chance that I might be Katy has my brain buzzing. Don't you think worrying about my parents is part of it? Right now I wish I hadn't come here."

"Well, then, forget the whole thing."

"I can't! I've tried and all I do is think more about it. I've been Chris Emery for as long as I can remember. But what about before? Being adopted, you just automatically have that question. I've always had it. And I want answers, but even so, the idea of maybe being Katy blows my mind."

"Why?"

"Because I'd be somebody else. And that's creepy."

"Maybe you'd like being Katy. Wouldn't be too bad a deal. You'd have lots of money."

"Money has nothing to do with it! Anyway, even if there's a chance that it's so, I'm not sure I want to be Katy."

"That's good," Tony said, "because I don't see how you could be."

"Are you saying I'm imagining it all?"

"Hey, don't get so steamed! What I'm saying is that if you were found around here, you would've been claimed for sure. In El Nido everybody knows everybody else's business. Especially the Teales and the Lessings. There is no way you wouldn't have been returned to them."

"But maybe I wasn't found right here. Maybe I wandered off. So maybe whoever found me didn't know me. Maybe I was kidnapped. Maybe, maybe, *maybe*! How do I know?" Her voice was stretched too tight, pitched too high. "Besides, what do *you* know about being adopted? About not having any idea who you really are? It's a terrible, gnawing kind of wanting to know. I've got some clues now. Maybe they won't lead anywhere, but I can't ignore them. I've *got* to find out what they mean!" She looked away, blinking furiously, then jumped up and pushed herself down the rocks, half slipping, half sliding until she reached the water's edge.

She shouldn't have talked to anyone. Tony certainly didn't understand. No matter what

Tony thought, everything added up. And something else: the weird way her mom had acted. She must have known something, something of importance, something to do with all this. She hadn't wanted Chris to come to camp. Was it because she had been afraid Chris might discover the secret of her past?

Chris blew her nose a couple of times before she turned and glanced up at Tony. He was standing, hands in pockets, staring over her head toward Camp Redoak, and he looked as miserable as she felt. It wasn't fair. None of this was his doing. She'd dragged him into it. She fought her way back up the slippery bank to the first of the flat rocks. Tony held out a hand and helped her the rest of the way.

Back on the bench he said, "I've been thinking. Guess you do have to find out what it's all about. If I were in your shoes, I would, too. So, if you want me to help, I will." He grinned. "But I still don't think you're Katy."

"I don't care what you think, so long as you'll help me!"

"Let's start with newspapers," he said. "The *Valley Courier* would have printed something about a lost kid. You know how they do. A picture with the caption, 'Does Anyone Know This

Child?' If they did, that'll end it, Chris. You'll know for sure you're not Katy.''

''Suppose that's so. Then how do you explain all the things that've happened?''

''Darned if I know,'' he said. ''But let's take one thing at a time. I'm going to be in town soon to get some stuff for the show, and I'll look up those old issues of the *Courier*.''

She nodded and said, ''Tony?''

''Yes?''

''If you see your aunt, or anyone . . . I wonder if you wouldn't . . . I mean—''

He put a hand over hers. ''I won't tell anyone. Not unless you say so.''

''Thanks.''

''Guess I'd better make tracks.''

Chris got up quickly, trying to ignore her disappointment. She'd had a strange feeling for a moment that he'd been about to kiss her.

''Hey, Becky!'' Chris called. ''Mitch asked me to talk to you. She wants to know about her cap. She says you took it at the tryouts.''

Becky aimed her thumb at the far side of the wide platform that fronted the dining room. ''I tossed it over there. Thought maybe she'd forget it.''

"Mitch? You know better than that." Chris walked to the edge of the platform and found the cap beneath the brush that spilled over on the cement. She waved it at Becky, and Becky gave a little snort.

"Can't imagine why she's so attached to that repulsive thing. Had it with her last year, too. But it didn't matter then. She only stayed a week."

"One week? Is that all?"

"One week. We thought she'd be here for the whole summer, but her folks came by late one night and, zip, Mitch was gone."

Chris felt the sting of anger. "Well, I hope this year is different," she said.

Becky started down the steps, and Chris, held back by two chasing campers, had to walk fast to catch up with her. She tried to sound casual when she said, "Say, Becky, does Doug work on the Grand Finale, too?"

"You mean because he was here with Tony? Uh-uh. He just likes to use the pickup." Becky gave her a curious look and said. "Matter of fact, I'm surprised he hasn't gotten next to Diane."

"Why?"

"Why not? She's got that wagon."

"He wouldn't do that, would he? Just use people?"

"If you say so," Becky said with a shrug. "Anyway, maybe he won't have to. Doug's a hunk. Diane'll probably make the first move."

Becky turned off toward the Lodge, and Chris walked on alone. Diane and Jan were the girls she liked the best at camp. Did they both have to be hung up on Doug? Apparently not, as Chris was soon to learn.

A couple of days later when she and Diane were on their way back to camp from El Nido Diane shouted, "Look who's there," and curved her car sharply into the lot of Pizza 'n More.

Six or seven umbrella-shaded tables were cemented into the ground to one side of the take-out window. On this hot afternoon all the tables were empty except one. Doug and two other Redoak counselors lounged under its red umbrella, drinking from tall paper containers.

Diane jumped out of the station wagon, marched to the order window and then to the table farthest from the Redoak three. It made Chris uncomfortable to act as if she hadn't seen them, but she followed Diane's lead. She sipped her drink slowly and stole glances at the guys over the edge of her cup.

The thin dark one was Ron Minter. He had been pointed out to her once when he'd driven by the camp in the Redoak van. The other was Sack Sorenson. And then there was Doug. He was laughing now, and his perfect white teeth gleamed in his bronzed face. She felt a smile on her lips and quickly bent over her drink to hide it. "Don't you even want to talk to the guys?" she asked Diane.

"You kidding? Of course I do. Something's wrong with my battery, and I've been trying for a week to bump into Sack."

So it wasn't Doug Diane was after! It was Sack. Out of the corner of her eye, Chris saw Sack lean back from the table and stretch. He got up leisurely.

"Hey, Diane! Hey, Chris!" he called, walking toward their table.

"Hey, Sack!" Diane said with a grin. "Is your mechanical know-how available? I've had trouble starting my car lately, and the battery's growing fuzzy white stuff."

"Corrosion. Come on. I'll clean it up for you."

Chris watched them walk away to the graveled parking area. A long shadow fell on the ground near her, covering her foot. She looked up as Doug sat down beside her.

"You've lost the wet look," he said.

She wanted to say something clever. Instead she struggled to keep her voice steady as she said, "How've you been?"

"Couldn't be better... *now*." Lowering his voice, he added, "Say, Chris, a bunch of us meet on the island once in a while to have a beer, or whatever... whatever turns you on. You know what I mean?"

"Island? What island?" she asked, stalling. She had a pretty good idea of what "whatever" was, but that didn't matter right now, did it? What mattered was that Doug was asking her for a date!

"Moon Island. Tonight. Why don't you come?"

"How? Swim?"

"No. I've got a boat. Pick you up at the big boulders." He leaned close to her. "I'll bet you'll look even prettier in the moonlight."

"What boulders?" she asked, afraid that the shakiness of her voice would give her away.

"Behind the last cabin, nearest the lake. You know."

She nodded but said nothing. If she moved, even so much as breathed, this lovely golden moment might disappear. She wanted to keep all of it: the hot touch of the sun on the tops of her feet; the warmth of the metal tabletop under her palms; the sweet Pepsi taste still left in her mouth. When the station wagon's hood slammed, she gave a little gasp and whirled around. Diane was handing Sack a rag. He wiped his hands on it, and they started back.

Doug whispered, "After lights out. There'll be another couple of girls. Will you be there?"

"I'll think about it," she said, "but I don't know."

Doug squeezed her arm. "Sure you do."

All the way back to camp something cold and uncertain prodded her. Whatever turns you on, he had said. And, of course, she understood. What else would he expect? In the next moment, remembering the sound of Doug's voice and the direct look of his blue eyes, she knew she would do it, no matter what.

"Hear you bumped into Doug in town today," Jan said later in the day when she and Jan were sitting on their cabin steps.

"Yes, we did. Not just Doug, though. Sack was there and that guy named Ron Minter. Doug's nice, isn't he?"

"Guess so," Jan said. "Did he invite you to the island?"

"Yes," Chris said, "but how'd you know?"

"A lucky guess."

"Jan . . . do you . . . do you mind terribly?"

"Mind? Oh, crumb! Is that what you thought? That I had a thing for Doug?"

Chris nodded.

"Well, I don't. Oh, I like Doug all right. I just don't like what he does. They've staked out the island, Doug, Ron and a couple of others, and use it for their parties. Last year, too. Everyone knows about it."

"I didn't."

"Well, you do now. I know it's none of my business, but what did you say to Doug?"

"That I'd think about it."

Jan slapped at a mosquito on her leg. "Think hard," she said, grinning.

When Chris left the cabin to meet Doug, Jan's remark was still rattling around her mind. At the boulders, she scanned the lake. Below her a stony ledge jutted out, and about three feet below that, the water lapped against the rock. She eased down to the ledge and stretched her leg, reaching until her toe touched water.

Behind her on the path, she heard footsteps and then a giggle. In the spin-off glow of a flashlight she saw Stacy and Val, the youngest of the assistant counselors. They were new this year, just like her, but, for some reason, she hadn't gotten close to them.

The two on the path had nearly reached her. They stopped. "Who's there?"

"Chris, Chris Emery."

"Well, what d'ya know?" Val said, flicking off the flashlight. "Never expected *you*. Who are you going with?"

There was no time for an answer. Stacy said, "Shhh! There they are."

From the lake came the sound of muted whistling. A couple of bars of, "Row, row, row your boat," repeated twice. Val and Stacy scrambled onto the boulder.

Chris heard a dull thud as the boat bumped the boulder, and then a boy's subdued laughter. "There's our catch for the night."

The two girls giggled.

"Haul them in." It was Doug's voice. "But, hey, we're not up to our legal limit. Where's Chris?"

"Waiting in line," Val said.

There was more laughter from the boat and a squeal from Stacy as she disappeared from the top of the boulder.

Val looked over her shoulder and whispered, "Come on, Chris, it's not a bad climb. Want a hand?"

"I'm not going," she said, taking a step backward. "Tell Doug I thought about it, will you?"

Chapter Six

Jan was asleep when Chris got back to her bed. In the morning Chris told her she hadn't gone to Moon Island.

"Thought I heard you on the trail," Jan said. "There was something for you in your box at the Shack. Did you get it?"

Chris hadn't, of course, but on the way to breakfast she stopped there. The folded paper in her box was a scribbled note from Tony. "Have something to tell you. Tomorrow, six-thirty. The Bleachers. Okay?" But even though Chris

gulped down her dinner and skipped dessert, she was late.

As she picked her way down the bank, she caught a glimpse of him through the trees. He was standing on the highest of the clustered rocks, throwing stones one after the other into the lake. When she reached the water's edge, she called to him and waved. He jumped to the lower rocks and held out his hand.

"Let me give you a lift."

"Thanks. Sorry I'm late."

"Are you? Doesn't matter." Tony scooped up another stone, and with a frown deepening on his face, hurled it far into the water.

Chris thrust her hands into her pockets and waited, watching a bird fly from the cove near the pavilion to land on the island. Finally she said, "Hey, Tony, what did you have to—"

He interrupted. "Hear you had a date with Doug last night."

"Sort of."

Tony's arm swung out, and another stone skimmed the water. "He sure got in late."

"I figured he would. But I had no way of knowing. I wasn't with him."

"Oh . . . but you had a date."

"Changed my mind."

Tony's face cleared. "Sorry."

"That I wasn't with him?"

"Cut that out, Chris. That I . . . well, that I—" He grinned. "Okay to forget it?"

"Sure."

Chris leaned over and gave his shirt a tug. "Hey, aren't you going to sit down? I'm dying to hear what you have to tell me."

He nodded and sat beside her. In a moment he took a deep breath and said, "Maybe this won't seem like news to you, but here goes. The old *Couriers* I looked at, those during and after the Great Meadows fire, didn't have a word in them about a lost kid. Nothing. Nobody was missing one, nobody found one."

"So what does that mean?"

"To me?" he said. "Not a heck of a lot alone. But when I found a picture of Mr. and Mrs. Lessing and Katy, I did a lot of thinking. That little girl sure looks a lot like you, Chris."

"Have you got it?"

"Sure. I photocopied it."

"Well, can I see it?"

"It's not a very good copy. To begin with, it's a newspaper picture, and not too clear a one at that, but I—"

"Tony, for Pete's sake! Where is it?"

He handed her a brown envelope.

She pulled out the picture and stared at it. The copy was dark and smudgy, but even so she recognized Caroline Teale-Lessing. There was a stocky man sitting on a love seat beside her, and on her lap, an oval-faced little girl. The little girl's hair was drawn back over wide-set eyes and held by a broad, flat ribbon across the crown of her head. Chris nodded.

"She does look like me. But then I'm everybody's look-alike. Granddaughters. Nieces. Kid sisters, too. Even so... Boy, do I feel like a yo-yo. One day I think I must be Katy, the next I'm happy because I'm not. And now back to maybe being Katy again. I need to stop bouncing." She stared at the paper in her hands.

"Well," he said, "what do you think? Don't just stare at it. Say something."

"Sorry, Tony. I drifted away." She handed the paper back to him. "What I was thinking was that in the picture of me we have at home my hair is short and straight, with bangs down to my eyes. Different from Katy's. Of course, they could have cut it at the foster home I was in."

"Where was that?"

"I don't know for sure."

"Well, it doesn't matter anyway. Somebody could have picked you up around here and taken you anywhere. What's bugging me is, what happened to Señor Marcos's wife?"

"I don't know," Chris said. "And that's just one of the things I don't know. But the things I do know work for me. I'm scared to say it, Tony, you know, what I'm thinking. Even thinking it makes me feel disloyal." She took in a great gulp of air. "I'd better say it, though. Tony, I'm pretty sure I'm Katy Teale-Lessing, even if you don't think I could be."

"Who says I don't? I was convinced before I got here. It was that picture. She not only looks like you, she is you. I've been giving it a lot of thought, and it all hangs together."

"You know what this means, don't you?"

"Sure."

"It means I'll have to do something about it, and I don't know what or when."

"Talk to your folks, of course."

"I don't want to, Tony. This is my 'standing on my own two feet' summer. And there are other reasons. Besides, this isn't the kind of thing you tell your parents on the phone."

"Then what are you going to do?"

"Don't know. Any suggestions?"

"One. Don't talk to anybody. Wait."

"What would I be waiting for?"

"Your cue."

"What do you mean, my cue?"

"Your go-ahead. Something always tells you when it's time to act."

"Well, I hope something does soon. I don't like waiting." Chris felt Tony's hand tighten over hers. She had just time to say, "Thanks Tony," before his lips met hers.

The little girl who brought the message said, "It's some guy. He said he'd hang on."

Tony. Chris raced to the Lodge and picked up the receiver, but the voice she heard wasn't Tony's.

"Where were you the other night? Thought we had a date."

"Doug. Hi. About the date, I said I'd think about it, remember?"

"So then, where were you?"

"In the Shack, thinking . . . and in bed. Look, Doug, what I thought about is . . . well, it's not you, it's . . . you know, the island. That's not my kind of thing."

Doug laughed, a short, sharp little laugh. "So what is?"

She was glad he couldn't see the hot blush that spread over her face. "Try asking me for a movie, or a coke, or even just a walk."

"Sure, sure," Doug said, "I'll do that." He paused. "You're unreal, you know? Like you're living way back when a beer was big stuff."

"Sorry," she said, and could have kicked herself. What was she sorry for? She heard him clear his throat.

"Just thought you ought to know I'm disappointed in you."

"Is that what you called to tell me?"

"Yeah, mostly. But I'm your basic optimist, Chris, so I'll try again. Call you sometime."

She was glad to get away from the phone, even though on one level she was glad that Doug had said he'd call again. Her feelings were still mixed up; the night before she'd fallen asleep thinking about Tony.

Tony's kiss had made her feel warm and ... well, welcoming, as if it had been something she had been waiting for. It had made her happy, bubbling, laughing kind of happy. They'd talked silly stuff on their way back to camp that afternoon.

"What's your favorite food?" he'd asked. "Pizza? Mine's strawberries. I could live on bread and water if I knew there would be straw-berries for dessert.''

And she'd agreed. She liked Tony. She trusted him. He'd advised her to call her parents. Should she follow his advice?

By five-thirty she had made up her mind. She would call them.

Her mother answered when she placed the call.

''It's Chris, Mom. How's everybody?''

''Chrissy! Oh, honey, it's good to hear from you. I knew you'd have to call. What's wrong?''

''Nothing's *wrong*, Mom. I called because I have something to tell you. Something impor-tant about this place and me.''

''What's happened?''

''Nothing's happened. Mom, if you won't in-terrupt, maybe I can tell you.''

''All right. I won't. Go ahead.''

''I'll try to begin at the beginning.'' Chris took a great gulp of air. ''Maybe Dad and you don't know this, but about thirteen years ago there was a terrible fire around here, and that's when—''

''We know about that fire, all right. I knew this would happen. Your nightmares are back again.''

''About the valley?''

''Of course. What else?''

The silence that followed could have lasted a lifetime. "Mom? Was this where you and Dad found me?"

"Around there, yes," her mother admitted.

"I thought so."

"All right, Chrissy," Mom said, her voice brittle and businesslike. "Tell me why you called. Do you want to come home?"

"Home? No. Why?"

"Because...because you're upset, that's why."

"*Me?* Hey, you're the one who's upset. Relax, Mom. I'm strictly okay. Haven't had a nightmare since I came here. And I'm having a great time. Honest, I am."

Chris could hear her mother's breathing at the other end of the line and then in the background the sound of the hall clock marking the quarter hour. Finally her mother spoke. "Maybe I was wrong about your going up there," she said. "I'm glad the summer has been fun. I just hope it stays that way."

"Everything's going to be fine, Mom." Before guilt could tie up her tongue completely, Chris changed the subject. They made plans for her mom and Susie to come up for the Grand Finale.

So that was that. She'd tried. From now on she'd wait until something told her it was time to make a move. Tony had been right.

But always, and popping up at the most unexpected moments, there was the problem of being Katy and what to do about it. Alone sometimes she would close her eyes and try to drift back to that time, the time when she had been Katy, to feel what she had felt then, to be her again for a moment. She would daydream, imagining her life as Katy: chauffeur-driven cars and pony rides and a gentle nurse named Celia, who rocked her and sang her to sleep. Those were sweet thoughts, and she might have spent more of her time daydreaming if it hadn't been for Tony.

He left notes in her box almost every day. Usually they were just one sentence long; sometimes one word. "Hal's Market has strawberries big as tangerines." "Hi!" "Rehearsal next Wednesday. How about a ride afterward?" And he made phone calls two or three times a week.

Doug telephoned once, too, but she was gone on a bus trip. For a couple of days she struggled with whether or not to call him back. When she finally decided that she would, the guy who answered the phone at Redoak said, "Sure, I'll get him.'' He returned in a couple of minutes and said that Doug must've moved on somewhere, but he wasn't too convincing. Funny, when she put the phone back on the hook, it was with relief. Not at all how she would have felt at the start of the summer.

July had whisked by like a bright yellow bus, leaving her behind. August was more than half gone, and her carefree summer, with getting Doug's attention as the main goal, was almost over. The people who had filled her mind for most of the summer had been Katy and Caroline Teale-Lessing; Tony, of course; lately, more and more often, Mitch.

Mitch was behaving like a good kid in all the groups instead of the moody imp everyone was used to. And, besides, she didn't seem to be underfoot anymore. To Chris that seemed too good to be true, and she worried about it a little. So when she came across Mitch on her next free afternoon, she was surprised.

Out of the corner of her eye, she had seen Mitch lying on her stomach at the end of the wooden pier. Mitch undoubtedly belonged somewhere else, but that wasn't what arrested Chris. It was the limp dejection of the little body flattened there.

"Hey," she called, "aren't you supposed to be with a group somewhere?"

Mitch raised her head without turning and nodded grudgingly.

"Well, where?"

"Swimming lessons, I guess."

By this time Chris was standing over her. "Then you'd better get back there. Val will be dredging the pool looking for you."

"No, she won't. She thinks I'm at the office."

"Doing what?"

"They telephoned. They're coming for me."

They. *Mitch's parents.* "Oh, no," Chris groaned. "When?"

"Tomorrow. And I don't want to go!"

"Did you tell them?"

"Sure."

"What'd they say?"

"Nothing. Just goodbye. That kind of stuff."

"Well, we can't just sit here. We've got to do something. What's the good of your being a princess if you can't do what you want some of the time?"

Mitch looked at her and shrugged.

"You *are* the daughter of a king, aren't you?"

Mitch gave the palest of smiles and nodded. Then, without warning, she began to cry.

Chapter Seven

Here," Chris said, handing her a tissue, "blow your nose. Come on. I'll walk you to the swimming pool."

"Why?"

"Just come on."

Mitch got up reluctantly. "Lesson's probably over."

"Doesn't matter. You'd better check in with Val." They took a few steps, and Chris said, "I'm going to the office. I'm going to get Miss Allen to let me call your folks. Is that all right with you?"

Mitch looked up at her with red-rimmed eyes. "Won't do any good."

"I didn't ask if it would do any good. I asked if it was okay with you."

"Go ahead," Mitch muttered as she left her and headed toward the pool.

Chris walked to the lodge and was raising her hand to knock on Miss Allen's door when she heard the word, "Katy."

The voice was Mrs. Lessing's. "It's the thought of Katy that's making it so difficult," she said.

Slowly Chris dropped her hand.

"So that's what's been going on." Margaret Allen's voice was firm but gentle. "Good God, Caro, it's time you let go. It's been over twelve years."

There was the whisper of a sigh, and Mrs. Lessing said, "I guess I'm more like Santiago than I've admitted. So long as the house is there, I have a link with Katy. It's solid, real. Nothing else is. If I only knew what happened to her." There was a pause. "The uncertainty is getting to me, Margaret, all the years of uncertainty. I'm doing foolish things. The demolition of the house was set for the end of July, and then August. Just yesterday I postponed it again."

"For heaven's sake. What good will that do?"

"I don't know." Mrs. Lessing's voice sounded weary. "I just know that seeing the hill empty will be hard to take. It'll remind me of how alone I am. Katy would have made such a difference."

"Nonsense, Caro. Stop suffering when you don't have to. Take a trip around the world. Or get married again. Better yet, do both."

There was a little laugh. "Maybe I will, maybe I will. But not yet. Not until I'm convinced that I know the truth about Katy."

Chris must have lost touch with time for a bit because the next thing she knew both women were at the door.

There was a strange look on Mrs. Lessing's face, and Margaret Allen frowned and said, "Why, Chris is something wrong?"

"No... I just wanted to talk to you. I'll come back later."

"It's all right. I have time now. Caroline, this is Chris Emery, one of our counselors."

"Of course. The girl with Tony Atkinson. That's why I seem to know you."

"I... I guess," Chris said.

Mrs. Lessing turned away from Chris. "Goodbye, Margaret. Thanks for the advice." She walked briskly across the lobby and through the outside door. *Don't go. Wait! I have something to tell you!* The words pounded inside of Chris's head. She took one step toward the door, then stopped, the blood pushing up into her face with embarrassment.

"Something is wrong, isn't it?" she heard Miss Allen say.

Chris turned slowly, forcing herself to think of Mitch and her problem. "It's Mitch," she said. "I guess I'm troubled about Mitch. You know, Michelle Jarmon."

"What about Michelle?"

"It's her leaving. Mitch is feeling miserable. You know how she tries to tough things out usually...well, she just couldn't. She's been crying. You know how excited she is about her part in the Grand Finale. It's only a little more than a week till the end of camp, and having to leave tomorrow is a real bummer!"

"I couldn't agree with you more. I called her parents." Miss Allen smiled. "Mitch has a reprieve. I haven't had a chance to tell her yet, but her father promised to let her finish out the camp."

"That's great!"

"I'm as pleased as you are, Chris. I was about to send for Mitch when Caroline dropped in. I'll do that now.'' She started to move into her office but stopped. ''How about you? How are things with you?''

''Things are okay,'' Chris managed. ''Okay, really.''

''That's good. Remember, my door is always open. Come to see me any time.''

Less than half an hour later Chris was high above the lake on the trail to the pavilion. A light rain had started to fall, but she ignored it and plodded upward stubbornly. She wasn't sure what was driving her, but whatever it was it had something to do with a worried Mrs. Lessing who didn't want to do anything until she knew the truth about Katy. And who knew the truth? She did, and Tony. There was no question about it. Hearing the conversation in Miss Allen's office was the signal Tony had talked about, so now she had to do something.

She pushed up the trail, slipping easily into a daydream where Mrs. Lessing, alone in a high-ceilinged library lit only by the flames of a roaring fire—who cared that it was August?—turned to find her framed in the doorway. ''Mother,'' she whispered, ''I've come home.'' Mrs. Lessing rose slowly, the disbelief on her face turning to joy. ''Katy, my Katy,'' she said, ''forgive me. I

NOW THAT THE DOOR IS OPEN ...
Peel off the bouquet and send it on the postpaid order card to receive:

4 FREE BOOKS
from

CROSSWINDS ®

An attractive burgundy umbrella FREE! And a mystery gift as an EXTRA BONUS!

FREE HOME DELIVERY!

Once you receive your 4 FREE books and gifts, you'll be able to open your door to more great romance, mystery and adventure reading month after month. Enjoy the convenience of previewing 4 brand-new books every month delivered right to your home months before they appear in stores. Each book is yours for only $2.25 with no additional charges for home delivery.

SPECIAL EXTRAS—FREE!

You'll also receive the Crosswinds Newsletter FREE with every book shipment. Every issue is filled with interviews, news about upcoming books and more! And as a valued reader, we'll be sending you additional free gifts from time to time—as a token of our appreciation.

NO-RISK GUARANTEE!

—There's no obligation to buy—and the free books and gifts are yours to keep forever.
—You receive books months before they appear in stores.
—You may end your subscription anytime—just write and let us know.

RETURN THE POSTPAID ORDER CARD TODAY AND OPEN YOUR DOOR TO THESE 4 EXCITING LOVE-FILLED NOVELS. THEY ARE YOURS ABSOLUTELY FREE ALONG WITH YOUR FOLDING UMBRELLA AND MYSTERY GIFT.

PLACE THE BOUQUET ON THIS CARD. FILL IT OUT AND MAIL TODAY!

CROSSWINDS
901 Fuhrmann Blvd.
P.O. Box 9013
Buffalo, NY 14240-9963

Place the Bouquet here →

YES! I have attached the bouquet above. Please rush me my four Crosswinds novels along with my FREE folding umbrella and mystery gift, as explained on the opposite page. I understand I am under no obligation to purchase any books.   245 CIW YA2C

NAME   (please print)

ADDRESS   APT.

CITY   STATE   ZIP CODE

Offer limited to one per household and not valid for present subscribers. Prices subject to change.

PRINTED IN U.S.A.

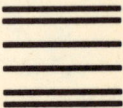

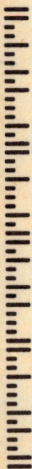

should have known you from the very first moment.''

But what if Mrs. Lessing laughed at her? Or what if she accused her of being an imposter? Of course she would know the truth the minute she saw the chain and the crystal heart, but they were back home in L.A. Becoming Katy wasn't going to be easy. There were all sorts of problems. The first was her parents.

How would they take it when she told them? Would they be sad? Would they refuse to give her up?

And what about herself? How did she—Chris—feel about it? For example her room. She didn't want to give it up. Some people might think that dumb, living in a mansion and all, but that room meant a lot to her. Mom and she had painted it, and Dad had built the bookcases just the way she'd wanted them, with a wide shelf for her stuffed animals. And there were her clothes. What a hassle it would be to clear out her closet! Of course Susie would be glad for it when she took over the bigger room.

Susie. Sure, Susie would be taking over everything, including Mom and Dad. She would have them all to herself. A sharp jab of jealousy jolted Chris, and she felt hot tears sting her eyes.

But enough of that! She paused and looked around her. She realized she was on the trail to Teale, not the pavilion. She gazed at the clearing just as she had done the first time. Today, however, she wasn't apprehensive. Today she wanted to find Señor Marcos. Eagerly she took the stepping stones to his door. She knocked, and when there was no answer, she went around the side of the cottage and found her way to the latticework gate and Katy's garden.

The grass around the swings was freshly cut; the flower beds, weeded. "Señor Marcos," she called, "Señor Marcos!" She waited a few moments and then took the lens cover off the camera and checked the light. A little breeze blew a straggly cloud away from the face of the sun. She made the appropriate adjustments and took two shots of the front of the playhouse, and then she had an inspiration. The pictures would be taken at the height of a little girl's eyes.

She was on her knees by the rear fence, taking picture number seven, a panoramic view of the whole place, when a wispy, unformed bit of memory touched her. It came and went—just like that!—and it left her heart pounding and her breath short. Yes, she had been here before. But, for Pete's sake, why was she so frightened?

She stared at the turrets of the big house. The memory had been elusive, but the fear was still with her, and when she heard footsteps at the gate, she was startled. It was the old man. "Hello, Señor Marcos," she called softly. "It's Chris Emery."

He scanned the yard, frowning.

"I'm by the back fence," she called, scrambling to her feet. "I didn't want to scare you."

"Ah," he said, "the girl with the camera." With garden clippers, he began to snip dead blooms from a flowering shrub.

"I guess I've taken all the pictures I need. Maybe I'd better be going," Chris said. He turned to look at her, and she said, "Señor Marcos, did Mrs. Lessing have any other children?" The question popped out of her mouth before she knew it was in her mind. "I know I seem nosy, but honestly, I have a reason."

"Curiosity is reason enough," he said with his surprising laugh. "*Es la sed de la mente*. It is the thirst of the mind. No, Mrs. Lessing has no more children."

"She's really lonely, isn't she?"

The old man's eyes left her face and circled the garden, resting on the long shadows made by the turrets of the house. "Night is coming," he said gently. "You must go."

"But Señor Marcos, it's early, it's only—"

"You must go!" he said impatiently. "You must not make me late."

"I'm sorry," she said, taking a step back, "I didn't know you had to be somewhere."

"It's not that I have to be somewhere, it's that I want to be. Mrs. Lessing permits me to have supper in the nursery, and Celia will be waiting." He smiled. "And then there's the little one. She hides, always behind the same chair, and I must go find her."

You don't have to go look for her! Chris wanted to cry out. I'm here! I'm here! I'm that little one! She wanted to run to him, to take his hand, but something held her back.

Señor Marcos returned the clippers to his pocket. "Go. It will soon be dark," he said as he turned his back and walked away.

"Señor Marcos, wait! Let me go with you!"

But the old man wasn't waiting for her. He was off through the gate and gone.

Chapter Eight

After rehearsal on Wednesday, when Chris met Tony by his pickup in the parking lot, she was thinking of Mrs. Lessing. As she slid onto the passenger seat beside him, she said, "I've gotten my signal, Tony. You know, my cue."

"Hey! What is it?"

"It's Mrs. Lessing," she said, and told him about the conversation she had overheard. "I can't wait, can I? I've got to tell her."

Tony brought the car to a halt by the side of the road. The hillside was rocky, and water made a pleasant sound as it trickled down the face of the rocks above them and disappeared.

"Sure you don't want to talk to your folks first?"

"I tried," she said, and haltingly described the phone call. She gave him a quick look. Had he changed his mind about her being Katy? Had he just said he believed it to go along with her? "I guess I don't want to worry them, not just yet. Besides, that was the sign, my go-ahead to do something, and it pointed to Mrs. Lessing. She's the one I should talk to.

"If you'd only heard her, Tony, you'd see what I mean. She's miserable not knowing. And, boy, do I ever understand that! When I was a little kid at places like the circus or Disneyland, I'd look at all the people's faces and wonder if that man, or that nice lady over there, didn't belong to me. Riding in a bus, sometimes, I'd stare intently at the people sitting across from me, hoping they'd recognize me and tell me who I was. Sometimes I thought they had, and then I'd realize that it was only wishful thinking. But I needed to know. It's important. Because you're never really complete, I mean, a whole person, until you know who you are." She drew in a great gulp of air and squared her shoulders. "Anyway, it's no fun wondering, and that's why I have to let Mrs. Lessing know."

"Can't argue with that," Tony said, and reached for the ignition. "I was going to take you to see Oakhill, anyway."

"Oakhill?"

"That's where Mrs. Lessing lives now. She built it after the other place burned." He turned the key, and the engine came to life.

They drove into El Nido. At the northern outskirts they turned a corner toward the hills. The narrow road lay between citrus groves, and the air was tinged with the fragrance of a few scattered blossoms. Soon they left the groves behind and curved through low, rolling hills dotted with oaks.

Chris sat back, relaxing for perhaps the first time in almost three days. Then, on a hilltop outlined against the sky, she saw a reddish-brown horse. When Tony said, "See that stallion? One of Mrs. Lessing's," she nodded and stiffened, remembering where they were going. After another half mile, Tony stopped the pickup at a pair of high wooden gates.

"Still want to go?"

"You think it's the wrong move, don't you?"

"No. But it's what *you* think that counts."

"Well, then I want to go—if we're not tres-passing."

"The gates are wide open, aren't they? No-body's ever kept out."

After a couple of more turns, they came to a long, grassy meadow. A large tile-roofed house backed up to the hills at its far end. Tony slowed down. "There it is—Oakhill."

"It's beautiful," Chris said.

A hint of a smile played on Tony's mouth. "Make you a bet," he said.

"What?"

"That strawberries out of season come with the territory."

"That's no bet. That's a sure thing."

Tony pressed the accelerator. The asphalt road cut straight across the meadow. The grasses on either side of them were the yellow-brown of summer, but Chris thought how it would look in spring, a broad expanse of brilliant green dot-ted, maybe, with wild flowers. Near the house the asphalt changed to patterned brick that swept in a broad curve to a high iron gate. Tony slowed down, then came to a halt behind a black lim-ousine that was stopped, waiting as some hidden mechanism slid the gate slowly into a deep brick wall.

Chris's eyes followed the disappearing iron-work. Then, with an effort, she looked at the rear window of the limousine. A woman wearing a pale blue hat was seated there.

Tony said, "What now?"

Her mouth was dry as sawdust, but she finally managed to say, "I guess we'd better say hello."

In front of them the chauffeur had his head out the window, eagerly waving at them to pull alongside. When the pickup stopped, Mrs. Lessing was leaning out her window, smiling up at Chris from under the broad-brimmed hat.

"Well," she said, "Tony and Chris. Dé jà vu. It's happened before, my coming across the two of you, hasn't it?"

Chris cleared her throat. "We were admiring your house. Tony brought me to see it. From the outside of course," she finished lamely.

Mrs. Lessing laughed. "The inside's worth seeing, too. Would you like to come in?"

Chris looked at Tony, and he whispered, "Go on. You'll never have a better chance."

They followed the black car into a parking area dotted with trees and shrubs. When the limousine disappeared around the side of the house, they parked and walked to a small wrought-iron gate set in more brickwork.

"Well, here we go," Tony said.

"Here we go," Chris echoed with a shaky little laugh as she rang the bell.

In a few minutes a tall woman in beige responded to their ring and led them through a flower-filled patio into the main hallway of the house. Mrs. Lessing was at a mirror, removing her hat. She swung around, her pale blue dress swirling gracefully.

"I've asked Miss Gale to show you around," she said, nodding toward the woman in beige. "When you're through with the rest of the house, come into the sun room. I can steal a few minutes to have a cool drink with you." She smiled, showing perfect teeth in a perfect oval face, and went up a curving staircase in the center of the hall.

She's like an ad in *Vogue*, Chris thought. She's so absolutely just right. She was still looking at the staircase when Miss Gale cleared her throat.

"Let's start with the small dining room," the tall woman said.

The inside of the house was all that the outside had promised: huge, high-ceilinged rooms with fireplaces; elegant furniture with just a touch of Spanish; glass doors and immense windows; plants growing everywhere.

One bedroom was in white, with touches of turquoise and pale yellow. A large recessed window that faced west had sheer drawback curtains and a window seat cushioned in turquoise. On the south wall a pair of French doors led to a small balcony that overlooked a swimming pool. Beyond the pool was a view of the high hills that bordered the valley and Oakhill.

"What a wonderful room," Chris said, returning inside from the balcony.

"It *is* pretty, isn't it?" Miss Gale said as she leaned over to smooth the pale yellow bedspread.

Chris could feel Tony's eyes on her, and when she looked up she found that he was smiling. Her feelings were showing, of course. *This was her room.* A shiver went up her back as she thought, Tonight, maybe she'll want me to stay here tonight!

In the sun room, Mrs. Lessing was seated in a cushioned rattan chair by a window that looked out on the swimming pool. Beside the window, French doors led to the pool area. She motioned them to sit in chairs near her and said, "There are cold drinks in the ice bucket."

They fussed around for a while, deciding on straws or glasses and ice or no ice. Finally Mrs. Lessing sat back and said, "Well, you saw the house."

"It's big," Tony said.

Mrs. Lessing smiled at both of them. "I know it is. Especially for one person. But I hope you also found it charming. I do."

"Who wouldn't?" Chris asked. She moved back off the edge of the chair and looked around, trying to find something of herself in this most lived-in room of all. On a far wall she found a family portrait: a man, a woman, a little girl seated on a love seat, just as in the newspaper picture. Tony, she saw, had found it, too. He looked from it to her, gulped down his cola and stood up.

"Miss Gale says you have two new horses. Mind if I take a look?"

"Of course not," Mrs. Lessing said quickly. "You know where the stables are."

Chris gave Tony a knowing look. You're doing it on purpose, her glance said. Clearing the stage for me, and I'm not really ready. He grinned at her. Go for it, his eyes said. Then he went out the French doors and headed for a gate at the far end of the swimming pool.

Chris twirled the striped straw in her can of Pepsi and wondered how to start.

Mrs. Lessing sat stiffly in the rattan chair, a frown coming and going on her face. In a moment she said, "I'm sorry. I was thinking of my daughter. She would have been a girl like you, and just about your age." Then her eyes glazed over with a look that said that she was far, far away.

She knows, Chris thought, *she knows.* She held her breath. Mothers always know their children, don't they?

"You're probably wondering what happened to my daughter," Mrs. Lessing said.

No, Chris wanted to shout, *I'm not! I know all about her! I am her!* Instead she leaned toward the woman and said, "I've heard about Katy...about the Great Meadows fire, too."

A cloud passed across Mrs. Lessing's eyes. "The fire, yes. I was in Europe when it happened. Still, I'd left Katy in good hands. With Celia. And there was Santiago, too." She straightened up, and her voice had a hint of defiance in it. "We traveled a good deal, but Katy never fussed when we left. She was such an easy child. Of course, she knew we'd be back. And, of course, she knew how much we loved her."

She's feeling guilty, Chris thought. *That's why she's saying all this to me.* Chris sat back in the chair, and as she did Señor Marcos came into her mind. She thought of how he had rushed to get to the nursery to play hide-and-seek with Katy. How he had told her about Celia, Celia who had rocked Katy and comforted her when the little girl lost her necklace. "Didn't you ever take Katy with you?" she asked.

The woman sighed. "Oh, we planned to. Of course we never had the chance."

Carefully Chris put the Pepsi can down and said, "I...I know this will sound crazy, Mrs. Lessing, but I'm your...I'm really your..." Chris bit her lip. Where was the ease of her beautiful daydream? *Mother, it's me. I've come home.* Why couldn't she say that?

Across from Chris Mrs. Lessing had tilted her head, and a little furrow deepened between her brows.

Chris's voice was shaking as she struggled on. "What you said about Katy, well it's not true...I'm here and...I'm...I'm..." She jumped to her feet, her face burning.

Mrs. Lessing looked at her watch. "If you don't mind Chris, we won't discuss my daughter anymore. I'm sorry I brought up the subject."

There was no use. She couldn't do it. She might as well give up. "I'd better go find Tony," Chris mumbled.

The woman stood up. Chris, already at the French doors, turned and said, "Mrs. Lessing, are you . . . are you by any chance going to the Grand Finale?"

"I expect so. Margaret will never forgive me if I don't."

"Good. Because my mother and father will be there." Chris knew what she had to say now—my parents and I need to talk with you, all of us together—but the words hadn't cooperated. They sounded like kindergarten sharing—at best. From the tone of Mrs. Lessing's voice, she must have thought so, too.

"Won't that be nice," the older woman said.

"What I'm getting at," Chris said, still struggling to make it come out right, "is that . . . well, that I'd like you to meet my folks. It's . . . it's important to me."

"How very nice of you to say that," came the cool, courteous words. "I look forward to meeting a good many of the parents."

Chris pulled at the door. "Thanks for everything," she said. Her voice cracked on the last syllable. Fool! What a fool she had made of herself! She ran out the door, slamming it behind her. In a few minutes she reached the driveway where the pickup was parked.

A while later, when Tony showed up, he hesitated, as if surprised to see her, but all he said was, "Ready?" On the way to the camp, he asked, "Aren't you going to tell me what happened?"

"Sure. But nothing happened. Not really."

"You mean you just talked about the weather?"

"We-ell, not exactly. She talked about her daughter, and when she did, I thought, here goes, but . . . but I just couldn't do it. Nothing seemed to come out right. Anyway, I'm going to talk to my parents first." She bit her lip, thinking she should say something more, but didn't know quite what until they had passed the small bridge where she had first seen Mitch racing by in her father's big car. "How could I possibly have thought to say anything to Mrs. Lessing before talking to Mom and Dad?"

"You didn't want to worry them, remember?"

"I remember. But how could I think that? After all, I'm their daughter and they're my parents, so it's their problem, too." She threw him a glance. "Go ahead. Say, 'I told you so.'"

"I told you so," he said with a grin. And then, "I'm glad you're going to wait. Maybe you'll relax for the rest of the summer."

"Guess so," she said, suddenly shy, her hands held tightly in her lap.

"Won't be much time to be alone with you, with the Grand Finale and all that."

"Guess not," she said, her voice small and whispery.

"Would you..." Tony gave his head a shake and began again. "Do you...do you want..." With a sudden quick twist of the steering wheel, he drove the pickup onto a small side road, then swerved onto a clearing. He turned off the engine. "Mind if we stop?" he said.

She shook her head and looked away.

Twilight was settling over the woods, giving the dry greens and browns of late summer a soft gray look. The dusky clearing had a hushed, breathless feel, as if, for a moment, all its creatures were holding their breaths, waiting...

She stole a glance at Tony. He was looking past her at the trees, and his face was thoughtful. And hers? Was it giving away how she felt? Tony stretched his arm across the back of the seat, and his hand, as brown as his face, ended close to her shoulder. She hadn't really looked at his hands before. They had a clean, able look, nice and masculine, with long, sturdy fingers. She turned her face away—just a bit; she was finding it hard to keep from brushing her cheek against those fingers.

Tony moistened his lips once or twice and finally said, "Chris?"

She looked up at him.

"Chris?" he repeated. "I . . . I want you to know I'm going to miss you—a lot. I sure feel as if I'd known you a long time. Guess that's because I think about you so much. I do most of the time, you know. When I'm working with the kids, when I go to bed at night, and first thing when I wake up in the morning. And that's practically all the time." His words came rushing out, stumbling one into the other. "I've never felt this way about another girl. Did I already say that? Well, anyway, I've never felt this way about anybody else. Have you any idea how much I . . . how much I . . . like you?"

She wanted to answer, but she couldn't. Then his face was close to hers. She sighed with pleasure as he kissed her.

Chapter Nine

Chris slid onto a bench beside Diane. "What's happening?"

"They're waiting for Mitch. Tony and Becky asked Jan to look for her."

"Why? Where's Mitch?"

"Who knows?" Diane said, stretching. "She hasn't shown up, that's all I know. So far they've rehearsed without her, but it looks as if they need her now."

Chris tried to remember if Mitch had said anything that would give a clue to where she might be, but she drew a blank. Should she help?

Then she saw Jan coming down the path, a red-faced, blue-capped little girl trailing behind her.

When they came near, Jan gave Mitch a little shove toward the platform and then slid onto the bench beside Chris.

Becky, at the far end of the stage, bent over and touched her toe in a graceful stretch. "Way to go, Mitch," she said icily, looking up. "Nice of you to drop in."

"Sorry, Becky," Mitch said. "Sorry, Tony. Guess we forgot. I'm sorry, honest I am."

"Don't waste time apologizing," Tony said. "We've already lost enough time. Let's just get started." He signaled the others to take their places.

"Where was Mitch?" Chris asked.

"Shuffling along the lake trail with Shana. Not a care in the world. Those two are as close as peanut butter and jelly lately."

"Always have been."

"Not like this. They've got something cooking."

"Maybe," Chris said. Early the next morning she remembered Jan's remarks.

It must have been near dawn, maybe four o'clock, when something awakened her. Little by little, she became aware of a series of little noises:

water trickling through the ancient plumbing under the floor beneath her bed, whispers, soft scuffling. Nothing unusual. The sounds were pretty normal for a dorm full of kids. She swung out of bed, pushed her feet into thongs and stole quietly through the dorm to the locker room door.

Outside, through the screened windows, she could see the night fading into a pale dawn. Inside, the dorm was in darkness. There were no unusual noises there, only the heavy breathing of tired little girls asleep. She moved quickly by the lockers and looked into the shower room. By the farthest washbasin, pointing a flashlight at something on its edge, were the shadowy figures of Mitch and Shana.

Mitch was whispering. "See? See how shiny it's getting?"

"Sure, I see," Shana whispered back. "But that's because I'm holding the flashlight, and I'm tired of it. I want to brush, too."

"It's not your turn yet. Besides, I found it."

"But it's my toothbrush!"

"Well, all right. But just for a little bit."

Chris stood still, pressed against the last locker, listening intently.

"Mitch," Shana asked, "d'ya *really* think it's gold?"

"Course it's gold."

"D'ya suppose there's more?"

"Course there's more. Nobody'd hide just one little chain. Wait'll we get way inside. We'll find all kinds of things."

"Not me. I'm not going inside. I saw enough."

"Chicken! Nothing in there to scare you."

"Yes, there is."

"Well, if there is, it's only because it's a real treasure cave."

Jan is right, Chris thought. They have cooked up something. That Mitch and her imagination! A treasure cave!

"That's enough, Shana," Mitch hissed. "Give it here. Gotta wear it under my shirt."

The beam of the light swung to the floor and against the wall, making misshapen shadows dance as the flashlight once more changed hands. Mitch grabbed a threadlike chain from Shana and pulled it over her head.

Shana pointed the light beam at her toothbrush. "Guess I can still use it."

"Course, you can. Come on."

Chris turned quickly and went back to her bed. Whatever those two were up to seemed harmless enough. Sure, she'd have to find out where they were making their "treasure cave." More than likely under a growth of poison oak. But so long as they didn't awaken everybody, let them have their secrets. What was camp without a secret or two? Especially when you could share them in the night. Susie and she had had them. And when Mom and Dad had sometimes caught them hopping about at midnight, they'd rarely been scolded. She was lucky to have both of them, especially now.

She stared up at the ceiling. Tomorrow, first thing, she'd write them. She'd even use one of those prefab postcards. She'd ask them to please come up early for the Grand Finale. She yawned and curled up under her light blanket. It had been a weird summer, she thought sleepily, and it wasn't over yet.

On Thursday, two days before the Finale, Chris saw a familiar figure down on one knee at the end of the boat dock. "Señor Marcos!" she called.

He looked over his shoulder. "There you are. You are the one I wish to see."

"Me?" she asked. "You came to see me?"

"Yes," he said, "and no. Your camp needs a new caretaker, and that is what I came for, but I also wished to see you. About the little one with the shabby blue cap.''

Disappointment and something like relief mingled in her tone as she said, ''Mitch? What about Mitch?''

He untied his boat, then turned, the worn gray rope hanging from his hand. ''She and the other small one, the one with the straw curls, spend too much time up on the hill alone.''

''How could they? We watch them all the time.'' Then, remembering Mitch's lateness at rehearsal, she grinned and added, ''You did say, 'kids have more ways to escape than a broken-down old fence,' didn't you?''

He nodded. *''Al buen entendedor, pocas palabras.''*

''There you go again. What does that saying mean?''

'''To one who understands well, few words are necessary.' ''

''I'll watch them,'' she said.

He muttered goodbye, stepped into his boat and, with the oars grasped firmly, moved swiftly across the water. She watched him until he disappeared into a far cove and then turned away. She would have to talk to Jan about Mitch and

Shana. If what Señor Marcos said was true, they were going much too far away from camp.

Late that afternoon, Chris was busy getting ready for dress rehearsal. The order had gone out the day before: "Everyone on stage at seven tomorrow. This is our one and only dress rehearsal!" Most of the Whiteoak counselors were in a utility room off the dining area, helping the kids dress and apply makeup. Chris was talking to a twelve-year-old girl.

"Keep your eye out for empty seats," she was saying, "and let Al, the fellow at the gate, know how many. He'll send another usher to lead the people here. Then you take over. Got that?"

Doug walked toward her. There was a flash of white teeth as he asked if she knew where Stacy was.

"Inside, helping with the makeup."

"Thanks," he said, and hurried past her.

That was all. No huge dramatic scene. The grand passion she had nourished most of the summer was as dead as last week's TV listings, and Doug, the object of it all, hadn't even known it existed!

When applause sounded behind Chris, she rattled off her final instructions to Al and hurried back to catch the show. She slid down a long row of chairs and squeezed into a seat beside Jan and Diane.

The show was a series of skits, sprinkled with songs and dancing. The acts were introduced by oversized signs on an oversized easel. From somewhere in the trees a circular spotlight zeroed in on the sign changes, but it wasn't really effective until twilight darkened the audience and the stage.

Through the thickening dusk, the spotlight flicked to a new sign, Sid, The Considerate Clown, and then to stage left where a little figure slowly climbed the broad stone steps. He was wearing a T-shirt and baggy trousers under a too-tight ragged black suit coat, along with enormous floppy shoes, a black derby hat and a cane.

"This must be new," Diane whispered. "Never seen it before, and I've been to all the rehearsals."

On the stage the little clown was playing games with the light, jumping out of its circle, making it chase him. He turned his back to it, bending over, peeking around and above his backside to wave with delight when he found it was still with him. Then he pointed to his chest with a questioning look. You want me? The bright circle moved up and down, yes, and with his hands the little clown pulled his frowning mouth into a broad smile.

"Who's that boy?" Chris asked. "He's good."

Diane said she didn't know, and Jan grunted. The little clown reached up to pull his hat firmly over his forehead and, although he caught himself almost immediately, Chris recognized the characteristic gesture. "Hey, it's Mitch!" she said.

"About time you caught on," Jan said. "Sure, it's Mitch. Tony's been working with her alone. Great, isn't she?"

Now a white-haired woman, one of the older campers with powdered hair, came onstage, struggling with a bag of groceries. The little clown hung his cane over his arm, tipped his hat and offered to carry the bag. The white-haired woman shook her head briskly, creating a powdery cloud around the two of them, and walked off the stage. The little clown shrugged, leaned his arm on an imaginary fence and crossed one foot over the other. From an inside pocket of his coat he brought out a banana and, with great care, peeled it halfway down.

He started to take a bite, but instead took a step forward, stretching his arm, offering the banana to the light. There was a soft, "Aw-w-w," from the audience. The spotlight moved right to left several times, and the little clown shrugged, went back to his unseen fence and proceeded to eat the banana. When he was through, he folded the peel neatly and tucked it into his breast pocket. Then he strutted to the edge of the stage, where he pulled a flashlight from his pants pocket and flicked it at the spotlight. Doubling over with laughter, he put the flashlight away and signaled the spotlight to come closer. He held his finger to his mouth as he looked over his shoulder. Then, leaning forward, he looked to the right and to the left. The little clown's shoulders drooped. He shook his head and, with his exaggerated shoes getting in the way, ran awkwardly to the far edge of the platform. He hesitated for an instant and then jumped, disappearing into the shrubs.

It was such an abrupt ending to the act that everyone sat silent for a moment. Then there was applause. The spotlight skipped uncertainly from the shrubbery to center stage, where it focused on Tony, who had burst into the scene through the dining hall doors. Even though she couldn't hear him, Chris could read Tony's words. "What's going on here, Mitch?"

She jumped up, scanning the area for Mitch. She was looking so intently for a redheaded clown who might be scampering clumsily up the walkway that she almost missed the white Cadillac. It wasn't hard to figure out what had happened. Mitch had seen her folks arrive and had run away.

Onstage Tony disappeared as quickly as he had shown up, and a new act started. Chris pushed through to the aisle. She could feel Jan moving behind her. Once out of the theater proper, they called Mitch's name softly, circling the dining hall. They went in through the kitchen and checked out the dressing rooms. No Mitch. They raced up the path to Cabin Twelve, but the rooms were empty.

Outside again, Jan said, "Thought her folks wouldn't be here till tomorrow."

"So did I."

Jan said, "She's got to be around camp some-where."

"Optimist." Chris looked beyond the paths and buildings of the camp to the moonless black of the woods. "I'll bet she'll run as far as she can get."

"In the dark? Wearing those shoes?"

"Sure. And wait'll I lay my hands on her." Chris swung around and pulled at the cabin door.

"Where you going?"

"To get a flashlight. Then up the lake trail. Not because I want to, believe me. Who'd want to hike uphill on a hot, humid night, fighting off mosquitos—"

"And bats," Jan said with a grin. "And all the other creepy things that come out at night. Hang on, I'll go with you."

Five minutes later they found Mitch's papier mâché shoe tops, dusty and misshapen, discarded at one side of the lake trail. Chris picked them up and put them on a log. "Mitch!" she called, "Mitch, it's Chris!"

There was a scurrying sound behind them. They played their flashlights in a circle through the woods and waited. Finally Jan shouted, "Mitch! Get out here this minute!" Again they waited, but they got no answer. The scurrying sounds were gone. Except for the stir of late-homing birds in the trees above them, the woods were still.

Chapter Ten

Jan almost stepped on the derby hat as it lay on its brim in the center of the path. She picked it up, brushed it off and hung it on a tree limb.

"Well, at least we're on the right track," she said, and they started up again on a trail that would have been invisible except for the two illuminated circles from their flashlights.

After a bit, Jan said, "Shhh. Stop a minute."

"What is it?"

"Don't know. Thought I heard something up there."

"If it's Mitch doing a number on us, I'll—"

"Shhh!" Jan flicked her light off, and Chris did the same. They stood listening in the sudden blackness.

"What're you trying to do, Jan? Scare me?"

"No, honestly. I thought I heard something. Guess it was just the wind in the trees."

Chris looked up through the quiet leaves above her, catching a glimpse of a star. "Come on, Jan, let's go."

They picked their way cautiously. The lakeside trail, familiar and friendly in the daytime, was tonight strange and treacherous, it's well-known landmarks transformed into dark, distorted shapes. When they reached the place where the Teale Mansion trail began, Chris said, "Look. Over there. There's the cane."

They put the cane on a boulder and began hiking up the hillside toward the old house. After a few minutes, Jan, behind Chris, tugged at her T-shirt. "There it goes again," she whispered. "Turn off your light."

"Okay, okay."

"Listen."

Chris heard shuffling, crackling noises, as if something was moving through the underbrush. "Jan! It's an animal! A bear, maybe!"

"No bears around here."

"Then it's a coyote."

"Maybe."

Chris held her breath, listening hard. Her eyes were growing accustomed to the dark again, and she looked carefully around her. Nothing. No sound now, no movement in the trees. Then below her, on the lakeside trail they had just left, she saw a light. At the same time above them, from somewhere near the Teale Mansion clearing, a man's voice shouted something and footsteps sounded on the path.

"He's after us!" Jan shouted, and they spun around and started sliding down the hill.

"Wait, Jan. I think it's only Señor Marcos up there."

"Sure, come on!"

"Listen. It *is* him. He's calling for Celia . . . and now for *chiquita*. Listen!"

"What are you babbling about? Come on!"

"*Chiquita*. He could mean Mitch."

"Forget him. The light down there is Mitch."

Jan pulled at her arm and, still in darkness, they slid and stumbled the rest of the way down to the lakeside trail.

When they got there, Chris snapped on her flashlight. "Why are we stumbling around in the dark? And why am I whispering? I'm not afraid of the old man."

"Forget him, will you?" Jan turned in a full circle, stopped and shook her head. "*Now* where's the light we saw?"

Chris aimed her beam ahead on the trail and then below them down the slope. The trees near the path were widely spaced, but closer to the lake the woods were thick and dark.

"Back to square one," Jan said disgustedly. "We've lost her again."

"Well, if she's not on her way to Teale, where's she heading?"

"The pavilion?"

"Could be. Let's look."

The bank was slippery. Even with their lights, they missed the path and slid on wet leaves and clay. They made their way slowly, clinging to boulders and pine branches that left a sticky, spicy smell on their hands. On the hill below her, Chris heard a sharp, swishing noise and then a groan and a curse from Jan. A yard or so later, when the branch of a sapling she used for support came back and slapped her on the face, she knew what had happened to Jan.

It would be a neat trick, Chris thought, if Mitch had made it down here in the dark. There was no sign of her in or around the wooden shelter.

"Mitch!" Chris shouted. "Where are you? It's us, Jan and Chris!"

"Come on, Mitch, answer us!" Jan yelled.

The night held no sound at all for a fraction of a second, and then above them, a man's voice called, "Over here, over here."

"It's Señor Marcos," Chris said. And then, "Okay, okay," she called, "we're on our way!"

Jan grabbed at her arm. "Do you *really* know what you're doing?"

"Sure, I do. He's okay. He's nice."

She heard Jan take a deep breath and let it out. "Either you're crazy," she said, "or I am, but, all right, let's go."

They stopped to catch their breaths a couple of yards from the lakeside trail. Above them, Señor Marcos waved his arms urgently.

"Hurry," he called. The meager glow of his flashlight seemed to thicken the shadows, and he appeared gaunt, grotesque, a scarecrow moved aimlessly by a night wind. "Hurry! They are up on the hillside!"

"It's all right," Chris whispered, and started moving toward the old man. She took his extended hand for the last couple of steps. Once on level ground, she said, "We're looking for Mitch, the little girl with the old blue cap. Remember?"

"The girl with the blue cap?" He sighed, a long, shuddering sigh and looked in bewilderment around him. "Ah, the little girl from the camp," he said finally, rubbing his temple. "So it is her light I saw on the hillside." He slumped against a tree, muttering in Spanish.

In a few seconds he drew himself up and said, "*Bueno*, let us not waste time. I know where that little one is going, but she is not a mountain goat, and the night is dark." He moved quickly up the trail, motioning them to follow.

At a point directly above the pavilion's roof, he turned sharply and began scaling the hillside, plowing his way through the trees. They followed, slipping and sliding on a deep cover of pine needles. After about five minutes of this stumbling climb under the pine trees, they came to an open space. Señor Marcos played his light on the hill above them. The trees had disappeared. The hillside that led from the open space seemed walled with rocks. The old man paused only for a moment and then started up the rocky slope.

They scrambled after the old man, always a couple of yards behind him as he wound around the rocks on some unseen path. Jan was having difficulty breathing, making peculiar crying sounds. But no, it wasn't Jan. Those sounds were coming from above.

"Help!" a muted, hollow little voice was calling. "Help!"

"Mitch!" Chris shouted. "Is that you?"

"It's me, it's me. Way up here!"

"Turn on your light. Where?"

Chris examined the rocky incline. "Hey! There she is!" She pointed high above them to a narrow beam of light coming from behind a great boulder.

"Okay, Mitch, we see you," Jan called. "Now come on down."

"I can't," came the shaky little wail. "I've tried and tried."

Chris turned to look for the old man and saw that he had gone on ahead. He was high above them, pulling himself onto a long, narrow ledge. On one side of the ledge, seeming to grow out of the slope, was an enormous boulder. From near its base streamed Mitch's ribbon of light.

"We're coming, Mitch," Chris called, then lowered her voice. "Hold the light steady, Jan. I don't see any footholds. How the heck did he get up there?"

They labored up the hill, and in a few minutes they were struggling over the ledge. Señor Marcos was bent over near to the ground, peering behind the boulder.

"There is no need to cry, *chiquita*," he was saying. "We will soon have you out of there."

On her knees, Chris crawled close to the old man and Mitch's light. She was looking through a narrow, almost triangular opening, its two sides formed by the hill and the boulder, its base, the ledge. "This is no bigger than a mousehole," she said. "How'd you get in there, Mitch?"

"Squeezed in."

"Well, squeeze out."

"Can't. Something's wrong. I keep getting stuck."

Jan tapped Chris's shoulder and said, "Señor Marcos is up on the higher rocks. Looking around, I suppose. Don't know what he expects to find. What's in there?"

"We know Mitch is. Let's see what else." Chris flashed her light through the slot and around Mitch as far as she could. "Hey, Mitch, looks like there's an opening in the hill to the side of you. What is it?"

"A cave. A treasure cave, I think."

"Well, if it's a cave, maybe there's another way into it. Why don't you take a look."

"It's probably full of awful things," Mitch said. "And it's all dark."

"But you have a light. Besides, Jan and I are right here. Go on, now." Mitch muttered something Chris didn't catch, but the glow of the flashlight moved away from the other end of the opening.

Behind her, Jan said, "Here comes the old man."

She turned as Señor Marcos stepped carefully down to the ledge. "There is no way to move that rock," he said, pointing toward Mitch's boulder. He snapped off his light, dropped to his haunches and sat, Indian-style, his back against the hill. "I must think," he said wearily.

Mitch called, "What're you guys doing?"

"Forget about us," Chris said. "You didn't take long. Did you even look in the cave?"

"Sure. Couldn't see much, though. Anyway, it's not really a cave. It's just a place between more rocks."

"You didn't look, did you?"

"Course I did." There was something in Mitch's voice that said otherwise.

"Try sliding out on your side," Jan said, and Mitch did, but that didn't work, either.

"I'll prob'ly be here all night." Mitch's voice was shaky.

"Hang in there, Mitch. It won't be long now," Chris tried to reassure her.

Mitch's folks would have the camp in an uproar. Probably threatening to sue. The whole thing was unreal. Chris rested her head against the hill and closed her eyes. Somewhere below them she thought she heard something, the rattle of stones, a faint call, and then, nothing. In a moment she turned to Jan. "What if we—"

"We've got to go get help," Jan cut in.

Chris nodded. Jan had read her mind. One of them should run back to camp. Alone on those dark, unfamiliar trails? There had to be another way. Maybe Señor Marcos would stay with Mitch, then both Jan and she could go.

"Chris? Jan? You guys there?" Mitch sounded frightened again. "You guys won't leave me, will you?"

"One of us has to," Chris said, standing up. "I'm going back to camp to get help."

"Be quiet!" Jan said suddenly. "I think I hear something."

"Here!" Jan yelled, jumping up. "We're up here!"

Below them a light appeared. "Chris! Jan!" The voice was Tony's.

"Up here! We've found her!" Chris scrambled to her feet and waved her flashlight.

By the time Tony neared their hillside shelf, all three of them were beaming their lights on the slope for him. Chris leaned over the edge and said, "Am I ever glad to see you!"

"Goes both ways," Tony said, and swung onto the ledge. "Good thing I saw your lights up here." He looked from the old man to Chris, and then to Jan, a puzzled expression on his face. "What's going on?"

"It's Mitch," Chris said. "She's holed up in behind that rock and we can't get her out." She pointed to the gap between the hill and the boulder. "Look for yourself."

Tony got down on his knees and looked into the opening. "What the devil are you doing in there, Mitch?"

"Who cares?" Mitch whined. "I just wanna get out."

"All right, all right. We'll work on it." Tony sat back for a moment, then he said, "You ever been in and out of this place before, Mitch?"

"Yes," the faint little voice replied.

"Okay, then, show me how you did it," Tony said.

Chris held her breath as she watched Mitch inch her way through the passageway feet first, her arms stretched above her close to her ears.

Jan said, "I don't believe it. As simple as that."

Chris put her arms around Mitch. "The important thing is she's safe," she said over her shoulder to Jan. Then she stood up slowly and put her hands on Mitch's shoulders. "You had no business running away!"

"You can say that again." Jan said. "And if you're not going to shake her, I will."

"No, no," Señor Marcos said from the darkness behind them. "The little one could not see what it was plain to see. She was frightened. She has suffered enough. Look at her. Her arms are all scraped and scratched from the roughness of the rocks. Are you all right, *chiqui*—" He broke off. Slowly he raised his arm and pointed at Mitch with a shaky hand. *"What is that?"* he asked in a choked voice. "What is that around her neck?"

Mitch shrank back against Tony. "What? What?"

Jan touched the gold chain on Mitch's chest. "This, sir?" she said. "It's just a necklace, a little kid's necklace."

"I found it in there," Mitch said, pointing to the boulder. "Do you want to see it close, Mister Marcos? It's got a flower on it, see? It's gold, too."

The old man bent over as Mitch pulled the chain up to her chin. "A single rose," he said, and Chris felt a sharp electric chill run up the center of her spine. "Yes, it is gold. A little girl I knew wore it around her neck." He straightened up and walked uncertainly toward the boulder.

"Hey, Mister Marcos," Mitch called. "What're you doin'? You're too big. You can't get in there."

"I know," the old man said slowly, "I know." He looked up at Tony and drew a long, shivering breath. "But my Celia could have."

Chapter Eleven

Celia again," Jan said. "What's he talking about?"

"Shhh," Chris said. "Let me think for a minute."

Tony walked over to her. "You okay, Chris?"

"I guess. But I'm mixed up. What does he mean?"

"Darned if I know. He's in and out of the past so much. Maybe he's just remembering."

"Remembering what? Should I go ask him?"

Jan took Mitch's hand and said, "Okay, you two. Talk all night if you want. Me, I'm taking Mitch back to camp."

"Good thinking," Tony said. "Otherwise you'll have the whole valley up here."

Chris went to the old man and pressed his arm. "Thank you for bringing us here, Señor Marcos." She turned to Tony. "If we go back to Whiteoak, will you stay with him?"

"Sure," Tony said. "I'll see he gets home."

Jan said, "Good. Now we're getting somewhere." She tugged at Mitch's hand, and they started down the slope.

Chris followed them. It was a tricky business, holding the flashlight in one hand, steadying herself with the other, digging in her heels wherever there was a firm foothold. She was glad when they finally reached level ground.

"Hey, there's my cane! Where's my other stuff?" Mitch asked.

"On the trail," Jan said. "We'll get it."

Mitch came upon her floppy shoe tops. She gathered them up sadly and grumbled, "They promised. They promised I could stay, didn't they?" Neither Chris nor Jan had the heart to reply, and they all walked in silence until they reached Camp Whiteoak.

Even from as far as the rise by Cabin Twelve, Chris recognized Sack bending over the footlights at the edge of the platform. Someone was waving a flashlight from the steps of Cabin Twelve. Its beam fell on them, and a voice called, "Holy Toledo, it's you, at last!"

It was Becky. "I see you've found Mitch. But where's Tony?"

"With Señor Marcos," Chris said.

"Something's wrong," Becky said.

"Nothing's wrong," Jan said. "Not with Tony, anyway." She sat down on the steps and rubbed her legs. "Boy, I must be black and blue all over."

"Well, you're in one piece, anyway," Becky said. "So the kids are all yours again."

Chris said, "What?"

"The kids. I've been sitting your crew. If they'd been left alone, Miss Allen would've gotten wind that you'd both gone."

"Thanks, Becky," Chris said.

Becky said, "Don't thank me. I didn't do it for you. I just don't want anything to spoil the Grand Finale." She gave Mitch a murderous look.

"Thanks, anyway," Chris said. She turned to Mitch. "Do you want me to go to the Lodge with you?"

Mitch's hand slid into hers and held tight. "Sure." She shuffled along, silent and sober, as they went down the path. As they neared the Lodge, Mitch's hand pulled away. "The car," she whispered. "The car. It's gone."

The white Cadillac was gone. Gone from where Chris had seen it last, pulled up carelessly alongside the Lodge veranda.

"They're probably out looking for you, Mitch," Chris said, tightening her grip on the little girl's hand. She squeezed Mitch close to her.

Miss Allen met them in the foyer. "Tony called from the caretaker's house," she said. "He told us Michelle was safe and sound and that you were on your way back." She steered them to the chairs by the fireplace and pulled Mitch down on the couch beside her. "Your parents were in a hurry, Michelle. Once they heard you were all right, they went on."

"Went? Where?"

"Why, San Francisco."

Mitch stiffened. "Then what'd they come for?"

"To ask if you could stay in camp an extra day. They can't make it back from San Francisco until Monday."

"Oh. Well, can I?"

"Of course, Michelle," Miss Allen said. "That's just how we arranged it."

In a voice that was barely audible, Mitch said, "That's good." And then, "I'm sorry I ran away. I know I made a lot of trouble for everybody. Like Jan and Chris..." She swallowed and added, "And Mr. Marcos, too."

Miss Allen raised an eyebrow. "Santiago Marcos? So that's why Tony's with him. What's wrong?"

"Probably nothing," Chris said. "But he was acting strangely and Tony thought—"

"He did the right thing," Miss Allen said, smiling. She rose. "Well, we'll forget the whole running-away business, Michelle. It was just a comedy of errors. Now, go on, girls. Go get your showers and some sleep. That's what I'm going to do."

Chapter Twelve

Chris waited until Mitch had showered and gone to bed and then went outside. She was too keyed up to sleep.

Beyond the outline of the shrubs by the path, deep shadows clustered, dimming the view of the boat dock and the lakeside trail. A thought struck her. Tony's car was in the lot. He'd be coming down that path to get it and then she could talk to him. She jumped up and hurried to the boat dock. There she leaned against a piling and frowned as she sorted through the events of the night. Finally she heard footsteps.

"Tony?" she called softly.

"That you, Chris? Still up? Good grief, why?"

She went up the path to meet him. "Couldn't sleep, that's why. Mind's whirling with questions... and... and things..."

"I don't think I'm going to be much help," he said quietly as they sat down.

Chris said. "Just... just listen, please. Something's really bothering me. Remember how I told you Señor Marcos said Katy had a gold necklace, but that I thought he was mixed up, that it wasn't gold at all, that it was silver and it had a crystal heart, that it was mine? Remember?" He nodded and she said, "Well, I was wrong about that, wasn't I?"

Tony nodded again but said nothing. Even the night seemed to be holding its breath. Chris drew in a great gulp of air. She put her hand on Tony's arm. "What I'm getting at," she said slowly, "is that they never found Celia or Katy... and... and... because of what happened tonight up on the ledge, I think I know where they are. Do you think the old man does, too?"

"Yes, he has it figured out pretty well," Tony said. "I'm glad you figured it out, too."

"Have we really figured it out, Tony?"

"What do you think?"

"It's just hard to change directions. All summer long I . . ." She shrugged in a gesture of defeat. "What's going to happen now?"

"Nothing till morning. I called my dad. He called the chief, then the chief called Señor Marcos. Looks like they'll move that boulder first thing tomorrow."

"And then?"

"Depends . . . you know, on what they find."

"I know what they'll find."

"Yep," Tony said. "Me, too."

They stared glumly at the dark expanse of gray that was the lake. Chris broke the silence.

"How is he? Señor Marcos, I mean."

"All right. Matter of fact, better than he usually is. He kept muttering something in Spanish about truth and *consuelo*. Finally he patted me on the shoulder. 'Truth has its own comfort,' he said. 'We will soon know the truth.'" Tony got to his feet. "And I'd better leave now. There are things I still have to do for the Finale, and with all that's going on, tomorrow'll be a crazy day." He bent over and brushed her cheek with his lips. "Night," he said.

"Night."

After he left, she moved to the edge of the wooden pier and hung her legs over the water. Tomorrow Mrs. Lessing would know the truth about Katy. Maybe it would be a comfort.

The dream was over. Chris looked up toward Teale Mansion, to where the trees blurred into a black sky. Nothing left but shadows. No more being Katy. No more thoughts of Oakhill. She swung her legs back on to the dock and pulled them tight under her chin as she grinned. No more strawberries out of season.

She stared at the calm, dark lake, trying to imagine the shapes of Moon Island and Camp Redoak and, to her right, the curve that led to the pavilion and its little bay. She was going to miss this place. Everything. Jan and Mitch. Diane. And, of course, Tony. They had been her summer family, the people with whom she had talked out problems and laughed laughs. That's what counts in a family, she thought, not just having the same blood.

She was an Emery as much as Susie was. Even if she had wanted to get out from under Mom's thumb. It had been time to be on her own. But not cut off. She never wanted to be cut off from them. She knew now that even if she had been Katy, that feeling wouldn't have changed. You just don't get rid of an old life the way you do old clothes. The Salvation Army doesn't pick up that kind of thing.

The air was getting cold; she hugged her legs tighter. She hated to go in. She was oddly comforted by the cool, dark expanse of water. Truth has its comfort, Señor Marcos had said.

Somewhere out here—in some far place, or even close by—there could be a woman who was her real mother, and a man who was her father, too. Who were they? What were they like? Would she ever, ever know?

Tony, looking worn and tired, drove into the lot with a truckful of costumes and props. When he located Chris, he took her aside. "Just heard from my dad," he said quietly. "They've dug into the hill, widened the gap and found what we both expected."

"That's pretty awful. Those poor people."

Early on Saturday morning Chris was called to the phone in the office. Her father was on the other end of the line.

"What's going on up there, honey?" he asked. "The news says that you had something to do with finding those people on the hill. Is that true?"

"I suppose it is. I guess I did have something to do with finding them."

"Well, well, my daughter, the detective."

"Detective? Not me. I wouldn't know a clue if it came up and bit me."

"Aren't you being too modest?"

"Uh-uh. You'll know what I mean when you get here. It's sort of a long story for now."

"It can wait. I just wanted to talk to you. And I'll see you today, anyway. About three. Okay?"

There was a long pause and then she said, "Daddy? You found me around here, didn't you? You know, before you adopted me."

"Why, yes, honey. We told you that long ago."

"Guess I forgot. Was it by the lookout near that castlelike place?"

"That's right. Why do you ask?"

"Tell you why later." Well, she thought as she hung up, if they told me where before, I guess the exact spot didn't matter to me then. It didn't matter at all until this summer.

At the foot of the lodge stairs, a group of girls had Mitch surrounded, and Chris sidestepped them. Mitch was the camp celebrity. The girls followed her everywhere, pounding her with questions. "Did you see them? Weren't you scared? Did you *really* find a gold necklace? Well, where is it then?"

Mitch had stock answers. "Course, I did. Course I wasn't. Course I found it, but he took it. It's circumstantial evidence. Besides, it belongs to Mrs. Lessing."

Chris and Jan were hounded by questioners, too. For the first few hours Chris didn't mind— too much—saying the same things over and over again. But it got tiring. After lunch she took her camera and bolted out of the Whiteoak gates and up the highway. Where the road curved, she turned and looked back at the camp.

As she watched, two women, Miss Allen and Mrs. Lessing, walked across the wide veranda and into the lodge. What was Mrs. Lessing doing there? Well, it was absolutely none of her business now.

She snapped one picture where she stood and then trudged slowly up the road, hugging the side as much as possible. She hadn't forgotten the near miss with Tony and his pickup at this spot. When she heard the hum of tires on asphalt behind her, she pressed against a boulder, waiting for the car to pass. Instead Tony's yellow pickup swung close to the slope on the other side of the road and stopped.

"So there you are," Tony called. "Want a ride?"

"Sure would. But what are you doing here? Won't the Finale fall apart without you?"

Tony shrugged. "Needed a break." He threw open the door. "Where to?"

"Teale Mansion," she said without hesitation.

They drove to Teale Mansion and stood by the stone fence at the lookout. Through a feathery mist that floated below them, Chris could see the roofs of the larger houses of El Nido and the white church steeple. And then the mist burned away in the hot noon sun and all of the village stood out in three-D on the valley floor. Tony sat on the edge of the fence while she took pictures. When she was through she sat beside him and told him about the call from her father.

"They found me right around here," she said.

"That figures."

"I'll bet I was the kind of kid Mitch is. You know, always running away. My real parents could have been camping near the highway. And if that's so, maybe I ran away and found Katy's play yard. I did remember it. And maybe, like Katy, my real parents didn't escape the fire. And they could have been from far away, so who would know to miss them, or their little girl?''

"You've got it all worked out," Tony said. "Again."

"I'm fitting together all sorts of iffy pieces, huh?"

He grinned. "Yep. Just like before, with Katy."

"No, Tony, that was special," she said in a quiet, determined voice. "That one really seemed to work. I was so sure I knew at last, and it was pretty exciting."

"I know," Tony said somberly, but his eyes held a teasing glint. "Stables and yachts—"

"And strawberries with cream every day," she finished for him. "But seriously, Tony, the excitement wasn't just about finding my real mother, even a rich one. It's pretty clear to me now that I didn't ever want to trade lives. I know who I am. What the excitement was about was finding something to get hold of, something of substance, not just shadows, to put in those miserable blank spots. The blank spots you lie awake and wonder about. Most people don't have them, Tony. Most people know their beginnings." She looked across the valley to the mountains and then down to the gray stone fence. "I . . . I'll just have to go on wondering."

Tony turned and took both of her hands in his. Steady, firm hands, gentle and warm. She looked up at him, and he said, "I wish I could help."

"You have," she said. "You are."

They sat silently on the fence, half facing the valley, half facing one another, the sun hot on their faces. There was the sound of a motor as a car went by on the highway, and the rustle of birds could be heard in the woods. Tony moved his hand, and the tips of his fingers touched hers. Then his fingers tightened over hers, and he stood up and pulled her to him. Tony kissed her, and his lips were warm and moist, his cheek firm on hers.

They walked to the car hand in hand. As they circled onto the highway, she glanced back at the towers of Teale Mansion. They'd be gone soon. A lump pushed its way into her throat, and she fought it back. She stole a glance at Tony, sensitive, suntanned Tony, and she wanted summer to go on forever.

He dropped her off at the Whiteoak gate. "See you after the Grand Finale."

"Sure. Mom and Dad'll want to meet the writer-designer-producer-director—"

"I'll be there," he cut in, and drove away.

She sat on a rock, watching the pickup until it disappeared around a curve in the wooded road. A few minutes later, a familiar black limousine drove between the gateposts and parked by the Lodge. The chauffeur got out, and in a minute the other front door opened and Señor Marcos stepped out slowly.

While the driver hurried into the building, Señor Marcos went up the steps hesitantly, waiting at the top. In a moment Mitch came out of the Lodge. She ran to him, and the sun glinted on a gold chain that hung from her neck. Katy's necklace. Mrs. Lessing must have given it to Mitch!

The chauffeur reappeared, holding open the Lodge door, and Mrs. Lessing stepped through. She walked across the veranda, paused an instant and then held out her arms to the old man.

Tears blurred Chris's vision. Quickly she brushed them away and focused her camera on the three people standing at the head of the Lodge steps. This was a summer she wanted to remember.

* * * * *

Take 4 Crosswinds novels
and a surprise gift
FREE
and preview future books each month.

That's right. When you take advantage of this special offer, you not only get 4 FREE Crosswinds novels and a surprise gift, you also have the chance to preview 4 brand-new titles—delivered right to your door every month *as soon as they are published*. If you decide to keep them, you pay $2.25 each, with *no shipping, handling or additional charges of any kind!*

Crosswinds offers a wide variety of stories about girls and guys you've known, or would like to have as friends, and who share your interests and concerns. And we haven't forgotten romance! Two of our monthly selections are always romances.

As a member of the Crosswinds Book Club, you will receive these four exciting books delivered directly to you. You'll always be among the first to get them, and when you take advantage of this special offer, you can count on not missing a single title!

As an added bonus, you'll also receive our Crosswinds Book Club Newsletter with every shipment. This newsletter gives you the inside scoop on future books and publishes interviews with your favorite authors. It also features a Book Club members Pen Pal Club and prints a special showcase column of reader submissions, queries, comments and letters.

Start with 4 Crosswinds novels and a surprise gift absolutely FREE. They're yours to keep without obligation. You can always return a shipment and cancel at any time.

To get your FREE books and surprise gift, fill out and return the coupon today! *(This offer not available in Canada.)*

════ CROSSWINDS ™.

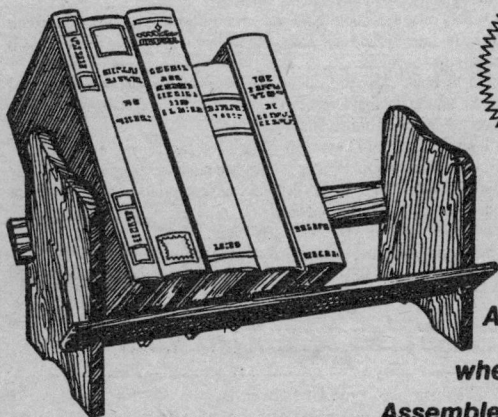